"You just can't accept it, can you?"

"Accept what?"

"That the woman exists who can find you resistible."

"Is that a challenge?"

"No, it damn well isn't!" Kerry said, furious with herself for getting involved in any kind of repartee with the man. "As I've said before, I'm here to work, not to play games with you!"

"I don't recall you saying that before. Not in so many words, at any rate." He was openly laughing, eyes crinkling at the corners. "I like your style, Kerry. So refreshingly astringent! Makes me wonder if that's the real you—or if there's a softer side underneath it all...."

"If there is *you're* unlikely to find it!"

"Now *that*," Luke returned, "is quite definitely a challenge!"

KAY THORPE was born in Sheffield, England, in 1935. She tried out a variety of jobs after leaving school. Writing began as a hobby, becoming a way of life only after she had her first completed novel accepted for publication in 1968. Since then, she's written over fifty books and lives now with her husband, son, German shepherd dog and lucky black cat on the outskirts of Chesterfield in Derbyshire. Her interests include reading, hiking and travel.

Don't miss any of our special offers. Write to us at the following address for information on our newest releases.

Harlequin Reader Service
U.S.: 3010 Walden Ave., P.O. Box 1325, Buffalo, NY 14269
Canadian: P.O. Box 609, Fort Erie, Ont. L2A 5X3

KAY THORPE

All Male

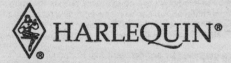

HARLEQUIN®

TORONTO • NEW YORK • LONDON
AMSTERDAM • PARIS • SYDNEY • HAMBURG
STOCKHOLM • ATHENS • TOKYO • MILAN • MADRID
PRAGUE • WARSAW • BUDAPEST • AUCKLAND

ISBN 0-373-11988-7

ALL MALE

First North American Publication 1998.

CHAPTER ONE

THE silver-framed portrait on the side table close by Estelle Sullivan's chair drew Kerry's eyes, making it difficult to concentrate on what the older woman was saying. It's subject was an assertively masculine face in its lean strength of feature, with a hint of sensuality about the well-shaped mouth. Steely grey in colour, the eyes seemed to be looking straight back at her, although they gave little indication of what their owner might be thinking.

Registering her distraction, Estelle turned her head to look at the photograph.

'My son,' she said with a hint of humour. 'He always did tend to draw feminine attention.'

And take advantage of it, thought Kerry with uncustomary cynicism, wondering if the connection had ever been publicised. Considering the amount of interest both mother and son had each generated in their time, it seemed unlikely to have been missed altogether—although the career paths were certainly far enough apart.

'A lot of media attention too,' she remarked on what she hoped was a suitably light note.

'One of the crosses the successful must bear with.' Estelle sounded a little cynical herself. 'Given the right kind of hype, this book may even put *my* name back in lights again for a while.'

'I shouldn't think there's much doubt of it. It's only been two years since your retirement from the theatre.' Kerry hesitated a moment, before tagging on diffidently, 'Did you consider making a come-back?'

Silk-clad shoulders lifted. 'If I were ten years younger

5

I might attempt it, but sixty is a little over the hill to start rebuilding a career.'

'Hardly from scratch. You're one of our finest actresses!'

Estelle smiled. 'Thanks for the present tense, but two years' rest makes a lot of difference.'

'I wouldn't call nursing a sick husband a rest exactly.'

'You give me too much credit. I was simply there with him. Others did all the work.'

'Being there is surely the most important part,' Kerry insisted. 'It must have meant a lot to him.'

'It meant a lot to me too. We had so little time together. These last six months have seemed an eternity.' The beautifully modulated voice became brisk again. 'One of the reasons I decided to write my memoirs. I've enjoyed an eventful enough life. Now that Richard's gone there's no harm in revealing some of the more spicy details from my past.' The last with a sudden roguish twinkle in her eyes. 'The only way to capture public interest these days.'

Kerry couldn't argue with that. 'How will your son react?' she ventured.

'Lee?' Estelle laughed. 'He's no angel himself!'

She wouldn't argue with that either, Kerry thought. At thirty-three, Lee Hartford was one of the country's most successful industrialists: a regular Midas whose every touch turned to gold. His turnover in women was legendary too. Almost every time one opened a newspaper, there he was with yet another in tow. Sarah was no doubt far from the only one to get hurt, though that made it no better for her. She still wasn't fully over him a whole year later.

'How long have you been with the agency?' asked Estelle, returning to the main purpose of their meeting.

Kerry refocussed her attention. 'Just under a year. I like a change of scene.'

'You've done this kind of work before?'

'No, but I'd enjoy the experience.'

The fine grey eyes twinkled again. 'That's what it's all about. When can you start?'

'Right now, if you like,' Kerry acknowledged, and elicited another laugh.

'Monday will be time enough. Lee is due back this morning. He's been out of the country this last week. Hopefully, he'll be coming straight on home from the airport.'

Kerry tried not to let her reactions show in her expression. Up until this moment it hadn't occurred to her that mother and son might share the same house.

'He insisted I come to live with him after Richard died,' said Estelle, as if guessing her thoughts. 'We get along well enough to make the arrangement work, although I'll naturally be moving out to a place of my own when he eventually marries. Not,' she added, 'that it's likely to be imminent. He's still far too fond of playing the field!'

'Does he know about the memoirs?' asked Kerry, not about to be drawn into any comment on that score.

'Not yet.' Estelle paused, appraising the vibrant face before her with its wide-spaced green eyes, high cheekbones and expressive mouth framed by the tumble of chestnut hair. 'Just as a matter of interest, did you ever consider doing photographic work? Your colouring is superb!'

It was Kerry's turn to laugh. 'I'm sure it takes a lot more than just colouring.'

'You have the bone structure too. A shame to waste it.' Estelle's voice became brisker. 'I've been jotting down notes for the last week or so, but they're very fragmentary. I thought if I just lay back and let it come as I recalled it all might be the best method. It can be revised afterwards. That's providing you can work that way, of course?'

'My shorthand should be up to it,' Kerry confirmed.

'Good. I did consider using a dictation machine, but they're so impersonal. I'll expect you to give me constructive criticism. Helen Carrington said you were extremely literate.'

'I read a lot, if that's anything to go by.'

'Biographies?'

'Among other things. I can't call myself a qualified critic.'

'Few critics can,' came the dry reply, 'but it doesn't stop them doing it. Your honest comment is all I ask.'

'You'll have it,' promised Kerry, trusting to the inner sense that told her the book was going to be a winner. This woman had led a full and fascinating life, with more to it than ever before publicised from what she had said earlier. There was nothing the public loved more than juicy revelation. 'Monday, it is.'

A long blue Mercedes was drawing up as she exited the house, slotting into the allocated space with dexterity. Dark-haired and powerfully built, the man who got out from the driving seat was instantly familiar. Taller even than his photographs suggested, Kerry assessed as he moved round the car: at least six-two. Caught on the step, she felt unable to simply walk away.

Lee Hartford eyed her with speculative interest, running a swift but comprehensive glance down her shapely length. 'Looking for me, by any chance?' he asked.

The depth and timbre of his voice was in total harmony with his appearance, striking a chord on her stomach muscles. A not unusual reaction, Kerry was sure, although she deplored it in herself. His business acumen apart, this man was everything to be despised in the male sex.

'I've been to see Mrs Sullivan,' she said levelly.

'Oh?' He waited, obviously expecting something more, thick dark brows drawing together a fraction when she failed to add to the statement. 'You know her personally?'

'No.' Kerry hesitated. 'I think it best if she tells you the whys and wherefores herself.'

The line between his brows deepened. 'Nothing wrong, I hope?'

'No.' Not from her point of view, at least, she thought. 'Purely a business matter,' she added.

'What kind of business?'

'It isn't my place to say,' she returned firmly. 'Good morning, Mr Hartford.'

He made no attempt to detain her as she moved purposefully down the remaining two steps, but she could feel his gaze on her back the whole way to the corner of the Georgian square, and was relieved to turn out of sight.

Brief though it had been, the encounter had ruffled her. Tall, dark and devastating was how one recent and obviously smitten journalist had described the man. What she had neglected to mention was his arrogance—his way of looking at a woman as if she were there purely for his delectation. Kerry could still feel the impact of those grey eyes assessing every detail of her face and body.

The antipathy he aroused in her was no surprise. Even without Sarah's experience to turn her against him, she would probably have felt the same instinctive dislike. How Sarah could have imagined for a moment that a man like that was to be trusted she couldn't conceive. His kind were takers not givers; one didn't need a degree in psychology to recognise that much.

The fact that he would possibly be around at times was certainly no enhancement to this job so far as she was concerned. On the other hand, she sure as hell wasn't about to turn down what promised to be one of the most interesting assignments she had ever been offered because of him. She would be working with his mother, not him.

As an actress, Estelle Lester—to give her her stage name—had rated high; as a character in her own right she came across as shrewd and intelligent, with an inner warmth that greatly appealed. Difficult to equate with the kind of man her son appeared to be. Other than the grey eyes, the only immediate point of resemblance between the two was in the dark hair.

Whatever the circumstances of the actress's first marriage, Kerry had never, so far as she could recall, seen or heard mention of the name Hartford in that connection. She did, however, remember the wedding four years ago with top-flight American attorney, Richard Sullivan.

Finding such a love so comparatively late in life, only to have it snatched away again so soon, was bad enough in itself, without the loss of a career. The memoirs were probably as much a means of reliving her life through her mind's eye as a potential money-spinner, Kerry reckoned. With Lee Hartford for a son, money could hardly be a problem anyway.

Cold and damp and gloomy, the day was typical of the time of year, making her thankful for the warm coat and high leather boots. With Christmas a bare three weeks away it might have made more sense to wait until the New Year to start this project, but hers was not to reason why.

Working for the agency this last year had proved infinitely more rewarding than the usual day-to-day routine all round.

The offer of a transfer three years ago to the London branch of the company she had worked for back home had seemed like manna from heaven at the time, but one office was much the same as another when stuck in it all day. Although life here obviously had a lot more to offer than the northern town where she had grown up, living it was also a lot more expensive. Profiles not only offered new interests, but a salary topping anything she had received to date.

The journey back to Battersea took appreciably longer than that coming out, due to some hold-up on the line. Off work herself, recovering from a bout of flu, her flatmate, Jane, was eager to hear how things had gone.

'Having his mother living with him must cramp his style some,' she commented when Kerry told her about Lee Hartford's surprise relationship. 'Although being an actress, she's probably a lot more open-minded than my mother would be. Judging from his publicity, he's a real womaniser,' she added slyly.

'I doubt if I'll be of any more interest to him than he is to me,' Kerry answered lightly. 'Hopefully, I shan't be seeing very much of him at all.'

Jane wrinkled her appealingly retroussé nose. 'Too bad. I had visions of a red hot romance!'

Laughing, Kerry threw a cushion at her before going through to her bedroom to put away her outdoor things. The full-length mirror in the wardrobe door showed a young woman in a grey jersey dress that skimmed the curve of her hips and emphasised her length of leg. Falling thick and heavy to shoulder level, her hair had a gloss that owed nothing to salon products, and the green eyes a healthy sparkle.

While suffering no false modesty regarding her looks, Kerry found them no particular asset either. At twenty-four she had almost given up hope of ever meeting a man as interested in her mind and personality as in her face and body.

It wasn't her intelligence potential Lee Hartford had been considering for certain, she thought drily, sitting down on the bed to remove her black leather boots. He saw women as good for one thing, and one thing only. Sarah could vouch for that.

She had shared this same flat with the other girl when she first came to London, until Sarah's modelling career had taken off with a bang and she had moved on to better things. Lee Hartford had picked her out at some promotional affair for one of his companies, and devoted enough attention to her over the next few months to convince her that he felt the same way she did. She had been devastated when he dumped her.

What a man like that needed was to have the tables turned on him, Kerry reflected. To fall, and fall hard for a woman and be treated with the same brutal contempt. She'd be the first to cheer such an event.

The weekend dragged, not least because Jane took herself off to visit her parents. Having been home herself a couple of weekends before, Kerry felt disinclined to fork out another substantial sum on rail fare so soon, especially when she would be going home for Christmas anyway. She settled for the usual biweekly phone call instead.

She spent Saturday evening having dinner with a man she had met during a previous job and been out with a couple of times since, but refused his suggestion that they go on to some party he had in mind on the grounds that she was tired. From his attitude, she guessed she wouldn't be hearing from him again, which didn't bother her a great deal. The relationship had been going nowhere she really wanted to be anyway.

Monday came as a welcome break. Estelle had requested that she reach the house around nine-thirty, enabling her to avoid the worst of the morning crowds. The gardens which gave the square its name looked denuded in the wintry sunshine, the trees stretching skeletal limbs. An expensive area altogether, the houses themselves were tall and white and graceful.

They were even more spacious inside than they looked from out here, Kerry already knew, the rooms being large, the ceilings high and ornate, the whole ambience one of tasteful affluence. Working in such surroundings was going to be a pleasure, she thought, pressing a finger to the doorbell.

Expecting the summons to be answered by the housekeeper who had admitted her on Friday, she was more than a little nonplussed when the door was opened by Lee Hartford himself. He looked arresting in a superbly tailored dark grey suit that defined his breadth of shoulder and lean-hipped build.

'Miss Pierson, isn't it?' he said on a formal note, contradicted by the faintly mocking gleam in his eyes as he surveyed her. 'Come on in.'

She did so, catching the faint scent of aftershave as she brushed past him. Yves Saint Laurent, possibly—expensive for certain. Nothing but the best for men of his ilk, of course, she thought caustically.

'My mother will be down in a minute or two,' he said, closing the door. 'In the meantime, I've been delegated to entertain you.'

'I'll be perfectly happy just waiting,' she returned, without looking at him. 'I'm sure you must have far more pressing matters to take care of, Mr Hartford.'

'None that can't wait.' He held out a hand. 'Let me take your coat.'

'Perhaps you'd just show me where to put it,' she said levelly.

'The independent type, are you?' He sounded amused.

Kerry kept her own tone even, her expression neutral. 'If you like to think of it that way. I'm here to work, not as a guest.'

'Fine.' If anything the amusement had deepened. 'In

that case, the cloakroom is over there. When you're ready I'll show you where you're going to be working. Mrs Ralston will be bringing coffee through in a few minutes.'

The cloakroom was almost as large as her bedroom back at the flat. Kerry slipped off her coat and hung it on a hanger, then took a swift glance in the long wall mirror.

The brown suede skirt and crisp white shirt looked businesslike without being overdone, the simple gold chain at her throat and small gold studs in her ears no detraction from the image she wanted to present.

She was wearing heels this morning for the simple reason that they looked better with straight skirts, but she was glad of the extra height. Not that she was small at five feet seven anyway, but that man out there made her feel so.

He was waiting in the wide hall when she emerged from the room. He ran another of those appraising glances over her, making her bristle afresh.

'Neat, and classy too,' he commented. 'My mother always did have good taste.'

'Mrs Sullivan hired me purely on the merits of my qualifications as a secretary, not for my appearance,' Kerry answered with a coolness she was far from feeling.

One dark brow lifted with a hint of sardonicism. 'Knowing her rather better than you do, I'd say both. You'll be working in her private sitting room, where the two of you will be undisturbed. You can use the study to type up the day's output. There's a word processor in there with plenty of capacity on disk.'

'You're not afraid of me breaking into your private files?' she asked with deliberation as he led the way.

'Not at all. They're safe under personal keycode. One

you'd be unlikely to guess if you tried,' he added. 'Not
that you'd learn anything of any use to you if you did.'

'Not that I'd want to,' she countered. 'Your affairs are
strictly your own business.'

A hand on the doorknob of a room towards the rear
of the house, he gave her a calculated scrutiny, taking
in the antagonistic spark in the green eyes, the jut of her
chin. An answering spark leapt in his own eyes. 'Very
much so.'

The message was clear, and not unmerited. Faint
though it had been, the innuendo had not been lost on
him. Kerry bit her lip as he opened the door and stood
back to allow her prior entry, aware of having allowed
antipathy to affect her better judgement. Other than
where Sarah was concerned, his affairs, business *or* personal, were of no importance to her.

The room was only half the size of the drawing room
where Estelle had interviewed her on Friday, but just as
beautifully furnished. The two deep chesterfields flank-
ing the Adam fireplace were covered in blue velvet a
shade or two lighter than the thickly piled carpet, with
cushions picking up the gold of the curtains. Delicate
water colours lined the plain white walls, and a baby
grand piano stood across one corner.

'Do you play?' asked Lee, following her glance.

'A little,' Kerry acknowledged, not about to claim any
degree of expertise, and added for something else to say
rather than through any pressing interest, 'Do you?'

He shook his head. 'My mother's the musician in the
family. If she hadn't gone into acting she might have
made a concert pianist.'

'She's very talented.' The admiration was genuine. 'A
great loss to the theatre.'

'There's no reason why she shouldn't start over. Her
agent already found the right vehicle for a come-back.'

'Perhaps it's just too soon,' Kerry suggested. 'She's been through a lot.'

The strong mouth took on a slant. 'More than the media would know, for sure.'

The intimation that she could have little idea herself was like a slap in the face. All she had meant to do was express sympathy. She took the chair he indicated, dismayed when he sat down himself on one of the sofas and lifted one leg comfortably over the other in a gesture that scarcely indicated an imminent departure.

'I'll be perfectly all right on my own,' she repeated. 'You really don't have to wait.'

His shrug was easy. 'I'm in no hurry. I understand your first name is Kerry?'

'Yes.' The skirt she was wearing had seemed conservative enough this morning at an inch above the knee, but it had ridden up when she sat down, exposing rather more Lycra-clad thigh than she felt comfortable with right now. She put down a hand to tug at the hem, desisting abruptly as the grey eyes followed her movement—hating the smile that flickered at the corners of his mouth.

'Nice,' he commented.

He could have been referring to the name, of course, but Kerry doubted it. There was even a chance that he imagined she was putting on a show for his benefit. Short of getting up again, there was little she could do to cover the exposed leg, which left her with no option but to ignore it.

'My mother seems impressed with you all round, in fact,' he went on. 'On the face of it, I'd go along with her—but, then, face values aren't always the best criteria.'

'Helen Carrington at Profiles will have already verified my qualifications *and* vouched for my character,'

Kerry returned tartly. 'You don't need to worry about my stealing the family silver!'

'*That* thought hadn't actually occurred to me.' He regarded her with quizzical expression, his gaze lingering on the full ripeness of her mouth for a moment. 'Are you always this hostile, or is it me in particular you're against?'

Already regretting the momentary loss of composure, she made an effort to sound properly repentant. 'I apologise. I was out of line.'

'I didn't ask for apologies, only explanations.'

'I don't have to explain anything,' she returned on as cool a note as she could conjure. 'I'm not in your employ, Mr Hartford.'

The glint in the grey eyes became a gleam, infinitely disturbing. 'You're in my home. That gives me certain rights, wouldn't you say?'

He was mocking her again, his whole manner nerve-jangling. Kerry steeled herself not to react, thankful when Estelle chose that moment to put in an appearance. Whatever her feelings toward the man, she would have done better to keep them under wraps, she reflected wryly.

'Sorry to be so tardy,' proffered the older woman. 'A few things I had to do before we get started. I hope Lee's been looking after you.'

'Oh, I have,' her son assured her. 'Kerry and I had a very interesting conversation.' The grey eyes turned her way again, the mockery still evident. 'You don't mind my using your first name?'

It took an effort, but she managed to keep her tone level. 'Not at all, Mr Hartford.'

'Lee,' he returned. 'Let's not stand on ceremony.'

Estelle looked from one to the other with sudden interest. 'Am I missing something?'

'Nothing of any importance,' Kerry assured her before

her son could answer. 'I'm ready whenever you are, Mrs Sullivan.'

The older woman smiled. 'As Lee just said, let's not stand on ceremony. Call me Estelle.'

Kerry smiled back. 'All right, Estelle.'

The door opened again to admit the housekeeper, carrying a tray. Lee got up to take it from her and deposit it on the table set between the two sofas, looking across enquiringly at Kerry. 'Black or white?'

It was already gone ten, she realised, catching a glimpse of the mantel clock out of the corner of her eye. By now he should surely be thinking about going to the office? The Hartford Corporation occupied several floors of a city high-rise, with a staff of several hundred; she knew that because she had worked there for a short period a few months back as a fill-in for someone off ill, although she had seen nothing of the company president at the time.

'Black, no sugar, please,' she requested.

'The way I like it too,' he acknowledged, pouring a cup and handing it to her. 'So we do have *some*thing in common.'

The only thing, she wanted to say, but with Estelle there she contented herself instead with a faint curl of her lip, not caring a damn if he saw it. Too late now, anyway, to pretend indifference. He already recognised her antagonism. If he proved curious enough to question further the source at some point, she might very well tell him!

Estelle took her coffee with a little cream but also refused sugar. Slim and shapely in cream jersey, she looked far from her age. She could play a woman in her thirties without any difficulty, given stage make-up and lighting, Kerry judged.

Her reluctance to return to the theatre seemed strange on the face of it. She had been such a star; she could so easily be one again. Her agent was obviously for it so why the hesitation? Surely not fear of failure? An actress of her calibre could never fail.

It was almost half past ten before Lee made a move at last.

'I'm playing squash with Phil early evening,' he announced, 'so don't wait dinner. We'll eat at the club.'

'Give Phil my love,' said his mother, 'and tell him it's about time he came over.'

'You could always pay him a visit,' Lee pointed out mildly.

'With Renata playing Lady Bountiful?' She shook her head. 'Not my scene, darling.'

The shrug held resignation. 'I'll convey the message.' He lifted a brief hand in Kerry's direction, the twist of his lips conveying a different message. 'Have a nice day.'

Estelle turned a speculative glance as the door closed behind him, registering the faint colour in Kerry's cheeks. 'I've a feeling you're not over-impressed with my son,' she said mildly.

The colour deepened a little. 'I'm sorry if that's how it came across.'

'You don't need to be. He can be pretty infuriating when the mood takes him. From the atmosphere when I walked in, I gather the two of you had been sparring?'

Kerry had to smile. 'I'd scarcely call it that. Just a difference of opinion.'

'A very big difference to put that spark in his eye. The only other time I see him look like that is when some business battle is about to commence. He thrives on opposition.'

'I can imagine.' Kerry reached for her bag and extracted her notebook and pencil. 'How would you like to start?'

It was Estelle's turn to smile. 'You're right, of course.

I'm procrastinating. Are you close enough over there if I stretch out on the sofa here and just start talking?'

'If I'm not I'll let you know,' Kerry promised.

Slipping off her shoes, the older woman settled herself comfortably with her head pillowed on a cushion. 'You've read a lot of biographies,' she said. 'Where would be a good place to start?'

Kerry considered for a moment before replying. 'Personally, I prefer the ones that go straight through from point A to point Z, rather than the flashback type.'

'From childhood, you mean?'

'If possible. Where and when you were born, what kind of lifestyle you had, schooldays and so on. Humorous little anecdotes, if you can remember any.'

'Plenty of those. I was always into mischief of one kind or another. I got myself expelled from my convent prep school for taking other pupils on guided tours of the nuns' quarters at a penny a time when they were supposedly all busy elsewhere. It was working quite well until we all trooped in on Sister Josephine who'd been taken ill and had had to retire to bed. I can still see her expression!'

'That's the kind of thing,' Kerry encouraged, laughing with her. 'What about your family?'

'I can't offer any rags to riches theme, I'm afraid. My father was in banking, my mother something of a society queen. We lived not very far from here in a house not unlike this one.' Her eyes were closed, her face relaxed, her voice reminiscent.

'My brother, Robert, was born when I was five. As a girl, I took something of a back seat from then on, I suppose. Not that it worried me too much. I'd had my first experience of facing an audience in the school Nativity play. I knew even then that it was what I wanted to do with my life...'

Kerry's hand raced over the page, her interest already

captured. Later they could go back over it all and perhaps insert a little more detail here and there, but for
now it was coming along just fine. She looked forward
to hearing more.

Lee Hartford she relegated to the very back of her
mind, vowing to keep him there from now on. He would
probably be spending little time at home during the day
anyway.

CHAPTER TWO

APART from a couple of brief encounters with the master of the house, when little more than a casual good morning was exchanged, that first week went by smoothly enough.

Working mornings only, Estelle was managing a fair output, leaving Kerry the whole afternoon to spend at the word processor putting the memories into readable form. What to keep in and what to leave out would be decided later. In the meantime, she was thoroughly enjoying the job.

She was in the study late on the Friday afternoon when Lee arrived home. With her back to the door and her mind absorbed, she didn't hear him enter the room, becoming aware of his presence only when he paused behind her to view the computer screen over her shoulder.

'So how's it going?' he asked.

His closeness disrupted her concentration, causing her fingers to stumble on the keys. Cursing inwardly, she deleted the mistyped letters.

'It *was* going fine,' she said pointedly.

He ignored the sarcasm. 'How do you rate it yourself?'

'On the basis of what we've got up to now, I'd say it stands an excellent chance of becoming a best-seller,' she answered with truth. 'Your mother has a way with words.'

'Part of what makes her such a good actress, I imagine. Words are her stock in trade.'

'Other people's words. These are her own.' Kerry

swung her head as he moved to the big mahogany desk a few feet away, meeting the grey eyes with that same involuntary tensing of muscle and sinew. 'Are you planning on staying?'

Dark brows lifted. 'Do you object?'

'Only in the sense that I find you a distraction.' She could have bitten off her tongue the moment she had said it, seeing his mouth take on the infuriating slant. 'The same way I'd find anyone a distraction when I'm trying to work,' she added swiftly. 'I realise it's your study, but you did say I could use it.'

'In your line you should be used to having other people around,' he returned. 'I've some work of my own to do, but I'm happy enough to have you share the premises.'

With anyone else there would be no difficulty, Kerry acknowledged. The best will in the world couldn't put her at ease with this man. Standing there in yet another of the beautifully cut suits—blue this time—he radiated a masculine air of command that set her teeth on edge.

'I'm just about finished for the day anyway,' she claimed. 'I'll leave you to it.'

He studied her thoughtfully, dropping his gaze to linger for a deliberate moment on the firm thrust of her breasts outlined against the cream silk of her shirt. 'We never met before, by any chance?'

She shook her head, making no effort to disguise her contempt. 'We hardly move in the same circles.'

'So you've based your view of me on what?'

Her chin lifted. 'You get a lot of publicity.'

'Oh, I see. My media reputation.' His tone was dry. 'You believe everything you read in the newspapers?'

Kerry gave him back look for look. 'I don't recall you ever suing any for libel.'

'So far I never felt any need. The people who matter

to me know me well enough to take everything said with a pinch of salt—the rest aren't important.'

'In which case,' she asked, 'why bother about my opinion?'

His smile was slow. 'You're another matter.'

'Meaning you're accustomed to instant idolisation from women?'

'I wouldn't go quite that far, but I don't usually elicit instant detestation either. How about giving me the benefit of the doubt and forming your own judgement?'

Kerry curled a lip. 'You just can't accept it, can you?'

'Accept what?'

'That the woman exists who can find you resistible!'

The smile came again, grey eyes acquiring sudden tawny lights. 'Is that a challenge?'

'No, it damn well isn't!' she said, furious with herself for getting involved in any kind of repartee with the man. 'As I've said before, I'm here to work, not to play games with you!'

'I don't recall you saying that before. Not in so many words, at any rate.' He was openly laughing, eyes crinkling at the corners. 'I like your style, Kerry. So refreshingly astringent! Makes me wonder if that's the real you—or if there's a softer side underneath it all. Be interesting to find out.'

Kerry took a hold on herself, aware of being got at. 'If there is,' she said with withering scorn, '*you're* unlikely to find it!'

'Now *that*,' he returned, 'is quite definitely a challenge!' Still smiling, he turned back to the desk and added over one shoulder, 'Make sure the heads are properly parked when you exit.'

'I always do,' she snapped, resenting both the instruction and the mockery. 'I've used computers before.'

'That's OK, then.'

Kerry was seething as she despatched the afternoon's

work to the printer, standing there and ostensibly reading the print-out as it emerged. Lee had taken a seat behind the desk and was going through some papers. She could see him from the corner of her eye, dark head bent, one lean hand wielding a pen—her presence obviously forgotten. He'd had his fun with her—that was all it had been—and now it was back to the important things in life. So far as she was concerned, he could go to hell!

With the hard copy safely stored, and both machines switched off at last, she was free to leave. It would be less than adult to stalk out without a word, she decided, and steeled herself to murmur a short, 'Goodnight.'

Lee looked up, his lean, hard-boned features illuminated by the desk lamp he had switched on. For a fleeting moment he appeared on the verge of putting some question, but the words didn't materialise. 'Have a good evening,' was all he said.

Estelle was watching children's television in her sitting room. She looked round without embarrassment when Kerry went in to take her leave.

'I adore *Blue Peter*, don't you?'

'I've never really watched it,' Kerry confessed.

'No, I suppose you're always on your way home from work when it's on.' She added unexpectedly, 'Why don't you stay and have dinner with us tonight? Lee will run you home.'

'It's nice of you to invite me but I have a date tonight,' Kerry improvised hastily. 'In any case, I wouldn't dream of dragging your son across town.'

'I'm sure he'd be more than willing, but if you already have an engagement...' The older woman paused, eying her speculatively. 'Someone special, is it?'

'Just a friend.' It was time to go, before she got herself involved in further lies. She gave her employer a smile. 'The hard copy is in the top drawer, if you want to go through what we've done up to now.'

'I think I'll leave it until we've got a bit further,' Estelle returned. 'I hope Lee didn't disturb you too much.'

'Not at all.' Another lie, but the only answer she was prepared to give. 'See you on Monday.'

Coming out of the cloakroom some minutes later dressed for the street in the camel coat which had cost her almost a week's salary, she was disconcerted to find Lee waiting for her in the hall. Leaning against the staircase newel post, he looked deceptively benign.

'I ordered a taxi for you,' he said. 'From now on there'll be one on tap every evening. All you have to do is make a call whenever you're ready to leave. The bill will be taken care of.'

A munificent gesture, Kerry was bound to acknowledge, though not one she cared to take advantage of, coming as it did from him.

'Thanks, but I'm quite happy taking the tube,' she said shortly.

The rejection made little noticeable impact. 'I'm more concerned with your reaching it safely. It's already dark out there. No time for a woman to be walking the streets on her own.'

'I've done it the past three years without coming to any harm,' she pointed out.

'Not in this area, with few other people about. Anyway, it's all arranged.'

She drew in a long slow breath, opposing the autocracy with every fibre. 'Do you take it on yourself to organise everyone's life for them? I don't *need* a taxi!'

'You're getting one, nevertheless.' Neither tone nor expression left any doubt of his adamance. 'My mother will be in total agreement. She said only last night that she worried about you leaving after dark.'

'Thoughtful of her, but—'

'But nothing.' This time there was a definite edge of

impatience to his voice. 'If you want to continue coming here at all this winter then you accept the situation.'

'Surely,' she said, 'that's up to your mother to decide?'

'Not in the circumstances.'

'Oh, I see. It's your house, and *you* make the decisions!'

'If you want to see it that way. Most people would be only too happy to have a door-to-door ride home at the end of the day.'

He was right there, but she wanted no favours from him. 'I'm not most people,' she declared frostily.

'Obviously.'

He had straightened away from the post, standing with hands thrust into trouser pockets and suit jacket pushed back to reveal a broad expanse of sparkling white. Kerry found her eyes drifting involuntarily downwards over the flat waistband and lean hips, warmth singeing her cheeks as she dragged her gaze forcibly upwards again to see his mouth slant.

'Devastating, isn't it?' he said softly.

'What is?' she parried.

'Sexual attraction. I was aware of it the moment we met.' The pause was meaningful. 'We both were.'

'There's such a thing as over-confidence,' Kerry retorted caustically. 'I'd say you had it in spades!'

'Uncertainty is no asset,' came the smooth response. 'If you weren't as drawn to me underneath all that antagonism as I am to you, you wouldn't be making such a song and dance about it.'

'I am not...' she began furiously, breaking off abruptly as she saw the glimmer in his eyes. It was all a big joke to him—a game he was expert at playing. The temptation to fling Sarah's name in his face was almost overwhelming. It took a real effort to resist it. Sarah herself might not want Kerry championing her cause.

The hoot of a horn from the street outside was something of a relief, despite her reluctance to accept the arrangement.

'I suppose that's the cab,' she said.

Lee inclined his head in ironic agreement. 'Let's not keep it waiting.'

He accompanied her out, opening the cab door for her.

'I'd suggest we meet over the weekend,' he said as she brushed past him, 'but I suspect you'd turn me down just for the hell of it. Maybe next weekend.'

Meaning that by then she would be bound to have mellowed towards him, Kerry assumed as he closed the door and lifted a hand in taunting farewell. Well, he could think again! Nothing he could say or do would change her opinion of him. It was set in stone.

Where her finer feelings were concerned, maybe, came the sneaking thought, but there was no denying her physical responses. Sexual attraction, Lee had called it: a chemical reaction that had nothing to do with liking or disliking. A governable one, though, she told herself tightly. When it came to mind over matter there was no contest. Not in this instance.

Phoning on the Saturday to announce her return from a two-week shoot in the Caribbean, Sarah sounded more up-beat than she had done in ages. Posing semi-nude for magazine and calendar work hadn't been her original aim, but the financial enticement had overcome any scruples she'd had. She had, she claimed, enjoyed the whole experience.

Kerry contemplated leaving Lee Hartford's name out of it altogether when detailing her own new job over lunch the following day, but the chance, no matter how remote, that Sarah might hear of the relationship persuaded her to come clean.

'He's everything you said,' she confirmed. 'Thinks he only has to beckon to have every woman falling over

herself to please him! It would do him a power of good
to have the tables turned on him!'

The vivacious face opposite hardened. 'It would need
someone capable of playing him at his own game.' She
gave a brittle laugh. 'If you feel the way you say you
do about him why not do it yourself?'

'Even if I were up to that kind of thing at all, I think
I've made my opinion a bit too obvious to start now,'
Kerry returned drily, aware all the same of a fleeting
temptation.

'You could always make out you were trying to cover
up how he really affected you. He'd believe it.' Sarah
was obviously taken with the idea, her eyes bright with
malice. 'You could do it. You could even enjoy doing
it! Just imagine the satisfaction you'd gain from giving
the great Lee Hartford the run-around!'

Kerry *could* imagine. What she lacked was the guts
to take him on. Fear of falling for him? suggested that
sneaky little voice.

'Not really my style,' she said flatly.

'It could be.' Having come up with the notion, Sarah
wasn't about to let it go that easily. 'You'd be avenging
all those he's made fools of, not just me.'

'You think he leads all his women to believe he's
going to marry them?' Kerry questioned.

'Maybe not all, but he definitely led me to think that
was where *we* were heading. Then suddenly it was over.
He just lost interest.' Sarah waited a moment, wry resignation overtaking the animation in her eyes when
Kerry remained silent. 'I suppose you're right. It wasn't
a good idea. Anyway, forget it.'

It would be a long time before Sarah was able to forget, Kerry guessed, sensing the depth of hurt still there
in her friend. Had there been any softening at all in her
own feelings toward Lee Hartford they would have hardened again. He was a total degenerate!

*   *   *

Monday morning was dry and sunny, the air crisp and clear. If only the winter weather could always be like this, Kerry yearned, walking from the station to the house with a spring in her step. The only drawback being, she supposed, that one would want to be outside in it rather than confined indoors.

In celebration of the sunnier outlook she had put on a skirt and matching waistcoat in a tan and cream checked wool, along with a cream cashmere sweater, the whole ensemble covered by a toning throw-over wrap. The outfit had drawn several approving glances on the way here, and drew yet another when Estelle saw her.

'You could stalk a catwalk along with the best!' she declared. 'I still think you're wasted doing what you do, good though you are at it.'

'I like what I do,' Kerry assured her. 'Although I'll certainly be sorry when this job is over.'

Estelle shook her head. 'That won't be for quite a time. I dare say there'll be a whole lot of revision to do before I can even think about submitting a manuscript.'

True enough, Kerry reflected, feeling anything but daunted by the prospect. If the bio failed to make the impact she predicted it wasn't going to be through lack of effort on her part.

That confidence faded just a little over the course of the morning when Estelle showed signs of having hit a mental block.

'I suppose I'm not really in the mood,' she confessed in the end. 'My mind keeps running off at a tangent. Supposing you type up what I've managed to come up with this far and see how it looks?'

Kerry did her best to hide her reservations. Running out of steam this early tended to suggest a basic loss of interest. It was possible that the whole autobiography idea had been no more than a passing whim on Estelle's part—a means of relieving the tedium. Her son was perhaps right in considering a return to the stage the best option.

She had almost completed transcribing her shorthand on screen when the telephone rang. She ignored it at first, trusting that Estelle would pick up the call, but it just went on ringing until she finally felt bound to lift the receiver herself.

'Sorry to interrupt the flow,' said Lee, before she could speak, 'but I've an urgent request to make. Can you spare Kerry to bring me the blue file I left on the desk? I need it urgently or I'd send someone out for it. A taxi should get her here within half an hour.'

'This *is* Kerry,' she said coolly. 'No one else appeared to be answering the phone so I took the call myself.'

There was a brief pause before he answered in an altered tone, 'Where are you?'

'In the study,' she confirmed, and heard him say something short and sharp under his breath.

'That's a separate line. My secretary got the wrong number. No matter. You're obviously not taking dictation right now so I'm sure Mother won't mind you bringing me the file. You'll find the taxi number on my desk pad. There shouldn't be any difficulty at this hour.'

Kerry bit back the rebuttal trembling on her lips. Estelle was paying her for her time. If there were any rebuttals to be made at all she was the one to do it.

'Certainly, Mr Hartford,' she said tonelessly instead.

She cut contact before he could make any reply. Not, she supposed, that he needed to say anything else. No byplay this morning, she noted. In all probability he had decided the game wasn't worth the candle where she was concerned. Well, that suited her fine!

As anticipated, Estelle was more than prepared to let her go, although she did ask if she minded. Kerry phoned for a cab, and spent the five minutes until it arrived touching up her make-up and running a comb

through her hair. If she had to do this at all, she told
herself, she was not going to arrive looking as if she'd
dropped everything to fly to his bidding!

The pre-luncheon traffic proved light enough to allow
arrival at the imposing tower block within the half-hour.
Kerry could have found her way up to the appropriate
floor but was bound as a visitor to report first to
Reception. The man on duty had her name already on
his list and sent her right up.

There were several other people waiting at the lifts,
among them a blond-haired young man she recognised
immediately though not with any particular pleasure.

'Who are you taking over for this time?' he asked
after they'd exchanged greetings.

'I'm not,' she said. 'I'm only here to bring Mr
Hartford a file he left behind.'

His brows shot up. 'You work for the big boss?'

'His mother,' Kerry corrected. 'I'd better get a move
on. He's in a hurry for it.'

The grin was meaningful. 'I'll bet!'

Kerry ignored the innuendo. It was what she might
have expected from Jason King. She'd gone out with
him once while she'd been working here, but hadn't
cared to repeat the experience after he'd made his interests only too clear. Yet another good-looking, out-for-
what-he-could-get dissolute!

He got off at the fourth floor, leaving her to continue
one more to the executive floor. She had never had occasion to enter the hallowed premises before, and was
tentative about it now as she approached the desk where
Lee's secretary held jurisdiction over further progress.

An attractive brunette in her late twenties, the latter
took the file from her with what Kerry considered an
unwonted chilliness in her manner.

'Mr Hartford asked that you wait,' she said. 'He'll be
through shortly.'

Kerry took the indicated seat with reluctance. He had better, she thought, have a good reason for keeping her here! She was going to be on the margin for lunch as it was: Mrs Ralston always served promptly at one. Hopefully, Estelle would be feeling more inclined towards work this afternoon.

'Shortly' turned out to be a good twenty minutes. Kerry sat fuming, on the verge of walking out by the time the inner office door opened at last. The two men who came out looked like bankers—an unmistakable breed in her estimation. Lee was right behind them, the meaningful lift of that mobile left brow as he looked across at her sending a sudden ripple down her spine.

'Sorry to have kept you so long,' he said. 'Come on through.'

She did so, weathering another somewhat frigid glance from his secretary. The kind of hostility that might be extended by the discarded towards the apparently newly favoured, Kerry conjectured, although she would have thought even Lee would draw the line at his own secretary, no matter how attractive.

The office was huge, with several easy chairs arranged in a casual grouping off to one side of the room, in addition to the usual accoutrements, and a stylish decor that managed to suggest affluence without being overdone. The window went almost wall to wall, affording a magnificent view out over the river.

'Impressive,' Kerry commented, refusing to be intimidated by it all. 'You really do yourself proud.'

'I get by.' Closing the door, Lee indicated the conversation area. 'How about a drink before we go to lunch?'

She looked at him sharply, taken aback by the casual statement. 'I didn't come for lunch.'

He returned her gaze equably. 'But you're here and it *is* lunchtime. I'd hardly send you back hungry.'

'I'd have been back by now if you hadn't kept me waiting,' she pointed out. 'If I'd realised—'

'If you'd realised you'd have given me the same cold shoulder you've been giving me since we met,' he interjected. 'It's time we came to a better understanding.'

Kerry regarded him in silence for a moment, registering the purposeful gleam in the grey eyes. The dark blue pinstripe he was wearing might give him an air of respectability, but underneath lay the soul of a born philanderer. As one who so far had shown resistance, she presented a challenge his pride wouldn't allow him to forgo.

So why not take up Sarah's proposal? came the sudden and reckless thought. Why not allow him to believe he was achieving a breakthrough? It would be immensely satisfying to lead him up the garden path, if only for a while.

'Your mother will be expecting me back,' she said with what she hoped was just the right amount of hesitation.

Lee shook his head. 'I spoke to her after you left and told her we'd be lunching together. She said not to bother going back afterwards. She'd prefer a fresh start in the morning.' He was moving as he spoke, crossing to a side table holding bottles and glasses. 'About that drink?'

Any vacillation she might have felt was swept aside by the sheer gall of the man. No matter what it took, she was going to give him his comeuppance, Kerry vowed savagely. Just see if she didn't!

'I'll have a mineral water, if you have it,' she said, and was gratified to hear how level her voice sounded.

'Ice and lemon?'

'Please.' Seated in one of the comfortable chairs, she watched him as he poured the drink, her eyes following the tapering line from shoulder to lean hip and assessing the muscular length of leg beneath the fine wool. Whatever his deficiencies in character, he was a perfect specimen physically, she was bound to admit. Fit as a lop, as her mother would say—although exactly what a lop was heaven only knew!

She lifted her gaze no further than the knot of his tie when she took the glass from him, trying to ignore the sudden tingle as his fingers brushed hers. 'Thanks.'

He was drinking the same thing himself, she noted in some surprise as he took a seat himself and lifted the glass to his lips—at least, that's what it looked like.

'I never drink alcohol when I'm driving,' he advised, correctly reading her thoughts.

'That's very responsible of you,' she murmured.

'A close friend was killed by a drunken driver only last year. I don't intend adding to the statistics.' There was no element of self-commendation in the statement. 'I gather the biography isn't coming along so well?'

'Just a temporary thing,' she answered, hoping she was right. 'I imagine most writers have their off-days.'

'You don't see her simply running out of steam?'

'Not unless she's in the habit of starting things she doesn't finish.'

'Normally no, but, then, she's never tackled anything like this before. How long are you supposed to be giving her?'

'It's an open contract. As long as it takes, I suppose.' Kerry directed him a contemplative glance, temporarily sidetracked. 'Do you object to the idea?'

The shrug was brief. 'Why should I object? It's her life, not mine.'

'But I imagine you'll come into it at some point.'

'Only on the periphery. The theatre was always the most important thing in her life. Until she met Richard, that is. And, before you ask, I don't have any hang-ups about that either. He was a good man.'

Kerry said levelly, 'She sacrificed an awful lot for him.'

'More than many women would be prepared to do, I agree.'

'More than *most* men would be prepared to do, for certain!' she flashed, forgetting the role she was supposed to be playing.

Lee gave her a quizzical look. 'You seem to have a down on men in general.'

'Not all,' she denied. 'By the law of averages, there have to be *some* good apples in the barrel.'

His lips slanted. 'Cynicism at such a tender age!'

'I'm twenty-four,' she felt moved to retort. 'Not *that* tender.'

'There's more to it than years. Judging from the way you've reacted to me up to now, I'd say you'd been let down rather badly in the not too distant past and tend to regard all men with a jaundiced eye.'

'Only those with the background to merit it,' she returned shortly.

He gave a mock sigh. 'And there I was thinking we were starting to make some progress at last!' He studied her for a moment, the smile still lingering about his lips. 'You're a very beautiful young woman, Kerry. Whoever it was who did let you down must have been mad. I'd say you could have just about any man you wanted.'

'Including you?' she asked with irony, and he laughed.

'I wouldn't say no.'

'With your track record, I doubt if you ever did!'

'My track record, as you put it, is a long way from what it's made out to be. I'd be clapped out by now if I'd had even half the women I'm supposed to have had.'

If she really did intend to play this game through she had to get back on track herself, Kerry reflected. 'You don't exactly go in for long-term relationships, though, do you?' she said, lightening her tone.

'Depends what you mean by long-term. One lasted several months.'

'She must have been something really special!'

'Very,' he agreed on a dry note.

'But still no staying power.'

He shrugged briefly. 'She started hearing wedding bells. I didn't.'

There was every chance that it was Sarah he was referring to, Kerry thought. Trust him to try making out it was all in her mind! Fired afresh, she concentrated on maintaining the banter. 'You intend staying a bachelor *all* your life?'

'Only until I meet a woman I can't live without.'

'Does such a being exist, I wonder?'

'I live in hope.' He was obviously amused. 'Whatever happens, I dare say I'll get by.'

'I'm sure of it,' she retorted tartly, losing sight of the object again for a moment. 'Money talks!'

She regretted the comment immediately, flushing a little as she met the grey glance. 'I'm sorry,' she said. 'That was out of order.'

He regarded her for a moment, his expression difficult to decipher. 'But not without some truth, all the same.'

There was a small silence, not—for Kerry at least—a comfortable one. When Lee spoke again it was on a dispassionate note. 'Talking of money, you could probably be making a great deal more yourself the way you look.'

'I've no interest in a career that relies on looks,' Kerry responded. 'I have a brain, too.'

'I wouldn't dispute it. But models aren't necessarily brainless bimbos either. The one or two I've been acquainted with were certainly astute enough.'

Sarah among them, she reflected—for what good it had done her!

'Obviously not enough to keep you interested,' she said.

'That's true. Maybe they were too predictable.' He glanced at the slim gold watch encircling his wrist. 'It's time we made tracks.'

Kerry's eyes were drawn to the well-shaped hand with its long, clever fingers. A good hand altogether—skin lightly tanned, nails smoothly trimmed. She felt a sudden fluttering deep down at the thought of those same hands touching her.

When he made love to a woman it would be with expertise, there was no doubt, but if what he had said a few moments ago was to be believed he had never experienced emotional commitment. Neither had she, if it came to that—regardless of what he thought—but they were far from being soulmates.

One thing was certain, she told herself determinedly, refusing to allow her physical responses to deter her from her aim, it was high time he discovered what failure meant!

CHAPTER THREE

THEY lunched at Claridge's. Not, Kerry believed, with any intent on Lee's part to impress her, but because it happened to be one of his normal lunchtime haunts. One of the perks that would no doubt be on offer if she carried this thing through, she supposed. Not that she considered it an incentive in any way.

Her host drew recognition from others in the restaurant, not least from one man seated at a nearby table who kept eyeing the pair of them throughout the meal.

'Kenneth Loxley,' Lee told her when she finally asked who the man was. 'He writes a gossip column for one of the tabloids. You'll probably figure in it tomorrow as my mystery woman.'

'Then perhaps you'd better explain who I really am,' she advised, trying not to sound too sharp about it.

'If he believed it he'd still make something of it.' Lee gave a brief shrug. 'It was probably a mistake to bring you here. I'm so inured to it all it never occurred to me to consider your side of things.'

'I suppose,' she said, 'that the women you'd normally bring here wouldn't be averse to a little publicity.'

He smiled faintly. 'You could say that. Would you like to leave?'

Kerry looked back at him with veiled green eyes, fighting the urge to say, yes, she would. 'It's a bit too late, isn't it? In any case,' she added with deliberation, 'I'm not passing up the sweet trolley. It isn't often I get to choose from an array like that!'

'It isn't often I get to lunch a healthy appetite,' he rejoined. 'It makes a refreshing change.' He studied her speculatively. 'Speaking of change, the aggression seems to have lessened—some of the time, at any rate.'

Patchy performance, Kerry warned herself. She would need to do better if she was to be convincing. If the truth were known, she was beginning to relish the game—one from which she intended to emerge carrying that dark head on a platter!

'I've decided,' she said smoothly, 'to take your advice and form my own opinion.'

'Well, good for you. The first woman I've met capable of taking advice!'

Light though it was, the taunt made her bristle inwardly but she controlled it, summoning a smile of her own. 'Maybe you just don't meet the right types.'

Lee laughed, drawing another conjecturing glance from the other table. 'Maybe you're right. So we start over from scratch, do we?'

'If you like.'

The grey eyes took on new depths. 'Yes, I do like—although I'll miss our spats.'

'What makes you think there won't be any more?' she asked blandly. 'I might form the same opinion I had to start with.'

'I'll have to make sure you don't.'

The arrival of the dessert trolley was a timely interruption, from Kerry's point of view at least. Playing this kind of game with a man of Lee Hartford's ilk might be a dangerous pastime, but it certainly gave life a little spice, she acknowledged, plumping for the succulent black forest gateau. She hadn't felt as alive in ages!

With no job to go back to, and animosity put on a back burner for now, she was in no particular hurry for the meal to be over. Nor, apparently, was Lee himself, although she had heard his secretary remind him of a four o'clock appointment when they were leaving.

It was gone two already, she noted, catching a glimpse

of his watch as he drained the last of his Perrier. The time had gone faster than she would have credited. In many respects he had proved himself an entertaining and stimulating companion. Too bad he was such a louse otherwise, she thought a little wistfully, viewing the firm features.

He looked up suddenly, catching her at it. Kerry felt the warmth under her skin, and knew from the quizzical lift of his eyebrow that her colour had risen. 'A cat may look at a king,' she parried, forcing a flippant note.

'Smart creatures, cats,' he observed. 'Would you like coffee?'

She shook her head. 'No, thanks. You must be wanting to get back to the office.'

'There's nothing immediately pressing,' he returned. 'I'll drive you home first.'

Green eyes revealed swift dissension. 'That really isn't necessary. I can take the tube.'

'Why do that when I have the car round the corner? Battersea, isn't it?'

'How did you know?' she asked in surprise.

'I rang Helen Carrington at Profiles that first day and asked for details. One can't be too careful when it comes to taking strangers into one's home.' Her expression brought a quirk to the corners of his mouth. 'Not my only motivation, I have to admit.'

Kerry kept her tone steady. 'What else did Helen tell you?'

'That you were one of Profile's most reliable people: intelligent, industrious and thoroughly trustworthy.'

'I never realised I was such a paragon,' she said drily. 'Maybe I should ask for more money.'

'Nothing ventured, nothing gained.' Lee took the pen held out by the waiter, who had just arrived with the bill, signed without bothering to check it, exchanged a few friendly words with the man then got to his feet to come round and take Kerry's wrap from the back of her chair, slipping it about her shoulders as she rose.

'No arguments,' he said firmly. 'I'm driving you home.'

Playing up to his masculine assertion was all part and parcel of the plan, Kerry reminded herself, swallowing a tart response. It had to be better than the tube, anyway. She summoned a bland note. 'You're the boss!'

His laugh was low, his breath stirring her hair and his hands lingering where they touched. 'Is that a fact?'

As he had said, his car was just around the corner. Only people with the luck of the devil could come up with a handy parking space in this area, thought Kerry, sliding into the soft leather passenger seat. They were out of time, too, she noted from the meter, but he didn't even have a ticket.

'I'm not always so fortunate,' Lee acknowledged when she mentioned the matter. 'I've been clamped on more than one occasion.'

'Then why not use taxis?' she queried.

The shrug was good-humoured. 'I hate being driven.'

'Better that, surely, than having to pay exorbitant sums to the clamping company—to say nothing of the waiting around?'

'I'm sure you're right.'

'But you'll still continue taking the risk.' It was a statement this time, not a question, her tone expressing her opinion.

He gave her a sideways glance as he started the engine, his eyes taunting. 'What's life without a little risk?'

Safe, it was on the tip of her tongue to answer, except that it sounded so dull, so unimaginative. She was taking a risk herself in leading him on the way she planned, if it came to that. Who was to say how he might react to the kind of put-down she had in mind for him?

She was jumping the gun a little, she reflected at that

point. One luncheon hardly established an ongoing interest. She stole a glance at his clean-edged profile, registering the sensuality in the fuller line of his lower lip and the strength of purpose in the jut of his jaw. Crisply styled, his hair was layered thickly into his nape, arousing in her a sudden urge to reach out and touch.

She was going to need constant reminders of the reason she was doing this, came the wry acknowledgement. His physical attraction was too obtrusive to be set wholly aside.

With the sun shining and the sky blue, Battersea looked more prepossessing than usual. Lee went straight to the right street without asking directions, suggesting that he'd probably looked it up on the map after discovering her address.

'Thanks for the lunch, and for the ride,' Kerry proffered as he drew up. 'I expected neither.'

'A small return for services rendered.' There was a brief pause before he added lightly, 'I wouldn't say no to a coffee to round things off.'

Kerry hesitated, torn between two fires. Common courtesy made a flat refusal difficult, but she was reluctant to be alone with him right now.

'*Just* coffee,' he added on an ironic note, watching her face. 'I never jump on a woman who doesn't want to be jumped on.'

'In that case,' she heard herself saying without having come to a conscious decision, 'by all means come up for coffee.'

Redecorated earlier in the year by Jane and herself in pastel colours, and with their own personal choice of fabrics at the windows and *objets d'art* around the place, the first-floor flat looked ten times better than when she had lived there with Sarah, but it still bore little comparison with what Lee was accustomed to.

The majority of the furniture came with the place.

Apart from adding a scattering of colourful cushions and a throw-over cover to the sofa, there was no disguising the general mediocrity.

Whatever Lee might think of it, he gave no indication. He seemed to fill the small living room with his presence.

'Have a seat while I make the coffee,' Kerry invited, dropping her wrap on a chair along with her bag. 'It will have to be instant, I'm afraid. We're right out of ground.'

'Instant's fine,' he said easily.

Instead of sitting down and waiting, he followed her to the tiny kitchen, lounging in the doorway while she put on the kettle and set out a tray.

She could see him on the periphery of her vision, his hands thrust into trouser pockets—pulling the material taut across his thighs in a way that tensed every nerve in her body.

Her hand caught against the rim of the jar as she spooned coffee, scattering some of the contents over the work surface and drawing an automatic exclamation of annoyance at her own clumsiness. It didn't help to see Lee's grin when she glanced round.

'Don't mind me,' he said. 'I'd have probably come out with something a whole lot stronger in similar circumstances.'

Kerry took care to keep her tone easy. 'Except that you're unlikely to find yourself in similar circumstances, of course.'

'Oh, I'm not beyond making myself a cup of coffee. I even cook a meal on occasion.'

She looked at him in surprise. 'When would you need to?'

'Mrs Ralston has all day Sunday off. Since Mother came to stay I've sometimes cooked for us both. She's

far from being the domesticated type.' The last without
rancour. 'Men make the best chefs, anyway.'

Kerry took that statement no more seriously than she
was sure it was meant to be taken. 'Of course they do!'

Lee quirked an eyebrow. 'It makes a change to have
you humouring me.'

'Just so long as you don't expect it all the time,' she
came back lightly.

'I wouldn't be so presumptuous.' He paused, viewing
her reflectively. 'Have we said a final goodbye to the
antagonism?'

Green eyes met grey, riveted by the sheer mesmeric
quality of his gaze. Kerry felt her pulse quicken, her
heart start thudding against her ribcage.

'It depends on whether or not you arouse it again,'
she murmured.

'I've still to work out just what it was that aroused it
originally.' He held up a hand as she made to speak.
'Don't give me that ''what you've read and heard''
story. You're too intelligent to take gossip column re-
ports on trust.'

'Perhaps you're giving me too much credit,' she said.

'Or perhaps it's because I remind you of someone
else?' he suggested.

Kerry reached for the boiling kettle, concentrating on
pouring the water without slopping it over the rim of the
cups. 'Like the man who supposedly let me down, for
instance?'

'It might explain your attitude.'

She could explain her attitude by bringing in a single
name, but that would finish the game too soon, she told
herself.

'If I've reacted differently today it's because you've
been different, too,' she prevaricated, leaving him to
draw his own conclusions.

'In what way?'

'Less arrogant, for one thing.'

'Arrogant?' The intonation was humorous. 'Is that how I come across?'

'Normally, yes. You're too used to dishing out the orders.'

'If you're referring to that taxi business I was simply being solicitous.'

'For my own good, you mean?'

'Something like that. You *are* going to take advantage of the arrangement, I hope?'

'I'd be a fool not to.' She softened her voice with deliberation to add, 'And I'm sorry for being such a boor about it.'

'Apology accepted.' He moved to take the tray from her as she lifted it. 'I'll carry this through. You just bring yourself.'

As she followed him Kerry found herself assessing the breadth of his shoulders again, visualising the rippling muscularity. No woman with normal reflexes could fail to be stirred by his sheer physical attraction, she acknowledged, but that was as far as it went. What he lacked, along with so much more, was integrity—in his personal affairs, at any rate. Business-wise, he appeared to be above board. At least, nothing untoward had ever been publicised.

It would look a little too pointed if she moved her wrap and handbag from the nearby chair in order to avoid joining him on the sofa, she decided on reaching the sitting room, although she wasn't entirely convinced by his earlier declaration.

'You have a good memory,' Lee commented as he took his cup of the black, sugarless liquid.

'Easy when you like it the same way I do,' she claimed without haste. 'Mrs Ralston's tastes better, of course. I shouldn't imagine she'd give house room to anything but the genuine article.'

'She might not. I certainly do. I'm all for the easy option.'

'I doubt that.'

Head back against the cushion and feet comfortably crossed, he gave her a deceptively lazy look. 'You don't really know me.'

'I don't know you at all,' she returned. 'Only, as you keep telling me, what others say about you.' She infused a tinge of regret into both voice and expression. 'Perhaps it's not all that fair to judge anyone on that basis alone, I admit.'

'So why don't we start afresh?' he suggested. 'Pretend we just met, and take it from there.'

Kerry regarded him with outward calm and inner turbulence, recognising the moment of decision. A part of her advocated retreat, but the retributory spirit still waxed strong. If she backed out now she would always regret the lost opportunity.

'I'd like to,' she said. 'Very much.'

He reacted as she had known he would, putting down his cup and taking hers from her. The kiss was light at first, a mere brushing of lips, deepening by degrees as he registered the response she couldn't have withheld had she tried. She could feel the hardness of his chest against her nipples, the spine-tingling play of his fingers at her back.

When he drew her closer still she went all too willingly, her arms sliding up around his neck on their own volition and lips parting to the silky pressure of his tongue. She had never known this intensity of enjoyment in a kiss. Her pleasure centres craved more.

It was Lee himself who called a halt, lifting his head to look down at her with an odd expression in his eyes.

'You're a whole bundle of surprises today!'

Kerry took control of herself with an effort, conjuring a flirtatious glint. 'Nice ones, I hope?'

'Sensational!' He lifted a hand and ran his fingertip over her lips, tracing the shape with a touch so delicate she could barely feel it. 'Utterly sensational,' he repeated on a softer note.

Every nerve ending sensitised, it took all her will-power to reach up and catch hold of his wrist. 'You're going to be late for your four o'clock appointment,' she got out.

Anticipating some degree of opposition, she was disconcerted when he capitulated immediately—kissing her lightly on the end of her nose before putting her from him and getting decisively to his feet.

'I'm going to be out of town for the next few days,' he said, 'but we could spend some time together at the weekend.'

To Kerry it sounded more of a statement than a question, suggesting a complacent reliance on her eager agreement and evoking a sudden resurgence of antipathy.

For a moment she was sorely tempted to tell him to get lost just for the sheer pleasure of seeing him deflated, but decided that the satisfaction would be too short-lived. He had to believe her ready to give him anything and everything he asked of her before she delivered the *coup de grâce*. Only that way would it reckon enough.

'Why don't we leave it till you get back?' she said. 'After all, something else might crop up before the weekend.'

'It would have to be something pretty urgent to change *my* priorities,' he returned. He stroked that same fingertip down her cheek and pushed back the tendrils of chestnut hair which clung there, his eyes holding hers. 'Till Friday.'

His technique was faultless, Kerry conceded grudgingly. He made every move seem purely spontaneous. She wondered if he kept a tally on how long it took him on average to get a woman into bed with him. He wouldn't be the first to cut notches, even if only metaphorical ones.

She stayed where she was for several minutes after the door had closed in his wake, aware of a deep-down urge to leave the whole business alone. Considering the response he had drawn from her just now, it was hardly wise to lay herself open to any further involvement.

Yet if she gave up so soon wasn't she saying in effect that she didn't have the strength of mind to resist him? she asked herself. That was something she couldn't and wouldn't accept!

She was busy preparing the evening meal when Jane got in at six-thirty.

'I keep thinking the rush hour can't possibly get any worse!' the latter declared, slinging away coat and shoes on her way to the kitchen. 'I left the office early tonight but it made no difference.' She lifted the lid of the saucepan bubbling away on the gas ring and took a sniff, making an appreciative face. 'Curry! Terrific! You must have been home quite a while to get this far.'

'Estelle wasn't in the mood so she gave me the afternoon off,' Kerry acknowledged, having already decided to keep the rest to herself.

'I thought authors had to be disciplined over output?'

'Only where they're reliant on the income, I suppose.'

Jane looked a little dubious. 'You don't think she's starting to lose interest?'

Kerry summoned a smile, lifting her shoulders in a philosophical manner. 'It's always a possibility.'

'You wouldn't mind?'

The shrug was repeated. 'There's never any shortage of jobs going at Profiles.'

'Not all like this one, though,' came the prompt rejoinder. 'Even fewer with someone like Lee Hartford on hand.'

'Hardly an advantage!' Kerry responded, and knew she had been a mite too quick when she saw Jane's eyes sparkle mischievously.

'Oh, of course. You can't stand the man, can you? Such an absolute rotter!'

Kerry had to laugh at the cut-glass accent. 'I'll bet it's no joke to those he's played around with.'

'Oh, he's probably not nearly as much of a playboy as the media make out. I mean, no man could be *and* run a company the size of Hartford's as well. I'm surprised you give it all so much credence yourself. You're not usually so easily influenced.' There was a pause, a sudden change of tone. 'Unless he's already started trying it on with you, of course?'

There was a time for truth and a time for prevarication, Kerry reflected, and this was definitely the latter. 'He wouldn't get very far if he did,' she parried.

Whether Jane believed it or not she left it at that, taking herself off to change her clothing for something more relaxed. Kerry stirred the curry and determined to put the whole affair aside for now. She had the rest of the week to formulate her plan of campaign. It might all fall through anyway if Estelle did decide not to continue with the memoirs.

Not in the least bit hungry after the lunch she had eaten, she had to force the curry down. Jane commented on her lack of appetite but was too intent on satisfying her own hunger to think anything more of it.

'One of the best you've done,' she declared with satisfaction when she'd finally had enough. 'I'll have to look to my laurels when it's my turn.'

With nothing else planned for the evening, they switched on the television, but soon grew bored enough to seek more mind-stretching entertainment in a game of Scrabble. It was in the middle of this, while searching for a letter which had gone behind the sofa cushion, that Jane came across the gold cuff-link.

With the engraved letter L staring her in the face, Kerry could hardly claim it as belonging to the only man she had ever invited to visit the flat, whose name had been Ray, and Jane denied ever having known anyone whose name began with L.

'It's Lee Hartford's, isn't it?' she said. 'He was here this afternoon, wasn't he?' She both looked and sounded injured. 'Why try making out you can't stand the man?'

'It isn't the way it might look.' Kerry took care not to overemphasise the denial. 'I took a file he'd forgotten to the office this morning, and he took me to lunch as a thank-you. He drove me back here afterwards and came in for coffee, that's all.'

'Then why keep it such a secret?' Jane wasn't about to be fobbed off. 'What really happened? *Did* he try something on?'

'No.'

'Then how come he managed to lose a cuff-link without even noticing?'

Kerry returned her friend's gaze with what equanimity she could muster. 'It must have just dropped out. I'll take it with me tomorrow. Are we going to finish this game?'

Jane took the hint with reluctance, obviously not convinced. Kerry could hardly blame her. Had the positions been reversed, she wouldn't have believed it either.

All the same, there was no question of telling her the truth. Jane would be the first to condemn the scheme. Sensibly so, too, she had to admit, but still couldn't bring herself to abandon the idea. This was as much for Sarah as anyone. If only by proxy, she deserved some redress.

Tuesday morning found Estelle in much the same frame of mind. After a couple of hours of almost total nonproductivity, she finally gave in.

'This is no good,' she declared wryly. 'We're getting nowhere fast. The whole idea was probably a non-starter. Who would want to read *my* life story!'

'Just about everyone who ever saw you on stage or in film,' Kerry assured her. 'The public in general are avid for inside information on the famous. Why else would the media go to such pains to fish out personal detail?' She kept her tone level, doing her best not to over-pressurise.

'You've had a fascinating life, Estelle. The kind few of us could ever hope to lead. All we can do is live it vicariously through people like you, who are willing to put it all down on paper.'

The older woman gave her a shrewd glance. 'Is that what you really believe?'

'Yes, it is.' Kerry was well aware of what lay behind the question. 'Other jobs may not carry quite the same kind of interest but I've never been out of work since I joined Profiles.'

'Of course you haven't. Helen said you were one of their most reliable people.' Estelle sounded rueful. 'I should have known better than to even think it.'

Kerry smiled a little. 'It's understandable. And I do want to carry on with this job. If you cancel the whole project I'm never going to know what your time in Hollywood was like, for one thing.'

'In that case, we'd better carry on.' Estelle was smiling too. 'You're very good for my backbone.' Stretched out on the sofa again, she added casually, 'I understand Lee is taking you to the Lattimers' party on Saturday evening?'

Too surprised to pretend, Kerry said blankly, 'I don't know anything about a party.'

Estelle twisted to look across at her. 'But he said it was all arranged!'

'Not with me.'

There was genuine puzzlement in the other woman's regard. 'Perhaps he intended asking you but didn't have time before he left. You do know he's away till Friday?'

'Yes.' Right then Kerry wished he would stay away for good. She made an effort to lighten both expression and voice. 'Who are the Lattimers, anyway?'

'Philip's an old friend. They were at Cambridge together. He inherited the family estate earlier this year, and married Renata not long after. They do a lot of entertaining. I'm sure you'd enjoy the evening.'

'I'm sure Lee can't be short of a partner to take.'

'I don't imagine he is, but you're obviously the one he wants to take—even if he did neglect to tell you about it.'

Kerry kept her eyes on the page in front of her. 'You've no objections yourself?'

'Why on earth should I have?' The older woman chuckled low in her throat. 'I can just imagine his reaction if I tried dictating whom he should or shouldn't take an interest in! He's gone his own way most of his life.' She settled herself more comfortably. 'So, let's try again. Only do tell me if I'm going into too much boring detail.'

Things went a little better from thereon in. By the time they broke for lunch Kerry had several pages of notes to transcribe. She found her employer's lack of egotism endearing. The vast majority of show-business personalities would take public interest completely for granted.

Lee was another matter. She hadn't anticipated him telling his mother of their association, especially when she hadn't even given him the go-ahead regarding the weekend herself as yet. He was so damned sure of himself!

All the more reason to bring him down a peg or two, she thought, firming her resolve. She would go to this party, she would give him every encouragement to believe her to be falling under his spell, she would keep on building his expectations for as long as she possibly could and then tell him exactly where to get off! The pleasure would be all hers.

The week flew by, not least because Estelle appeared to have regained her enthusiasm for the memoirs. Kerry continued to take advantage of the taxi ride each evening because she would, as she herself had said, have been a fool to refuse it, and was bound to acknowledge the advantage. Jane was openly envious. She only wished her boss was as thoughtful, she said plaintively.

It was on the tip of Kerry's tongue to point out sharply that Lee Hartford wasn't her boss, but she bit it back. Since Monday evening she had taken pains not to mention Lee at all.

It was hardly going to be possible to keep Jane in the dark completely if she started seeing him on a personal basis, of course, but she wouldn't be letting her in on the scheme until it was all over. By then it would be too late for any remonstrations.

Lee arrived late Friday afternoon. Printing out hard copy in the study, Kerry became aware of his arrival only when his lips touched her nape—startling her so much she thought her heart was going to leap right out of her mouth.

'Your hair had parted,' he said softly. 'An open temptation.'

She took a hold on herself, swinging to look at him with a deliberately provocative little smile. 'And you could never resist temptation, of course!'

'Not when it comes so deliciously presented.' Tall, lean, and wholly riveting in silver grey, he viewed her upturned features with a look in his eyes which left no doubt at all of his interest. 'You've been on my mind a lot these last few days. A real distraction!'

'I'd doubt if it proved to be any big problem,' she responded.

'Oh, but it did. You've been proving to be a problem for the last two weeks.' His voice was a caress in itself, the curve of his lips a reminder of how they had felt on her skin. 'One glance from those eyes of yours, and I was felled!'

'Cut down in your prime,' Kerry sympathised.

'What better time?' He paused. 'About the week-end—'

'I'm reliably informed by your mother that you intend taking me to some party,' she interrupted with purpose.

If he was discomfited at all he didn't show it. 'She asked me what I had planned for the weekend. I saw no reason not to tell her. If you don't like the idea we can always do something else.'

Kerry felt both inner and outer composure start to dwindle as she gazed at him. She could see the faint five o'clock shadow along his jawline, and knew an almost irresistible urge to run her fingers over it. His closeness assailed her senses, starting a slow burn down deep. Her limbs seemed to have lost all motor power.

Lee slid both hands up her arms to draw her closer still, each and every finger a separate source of heat melting its way through the fine material of her blouse. As before, his mouth was light on hers at first, lips brushing, beguiling, kindling a response she couldn't— and at that moment didn't even want to—control. She was lost in a world of sheer sensual pleasure, all coherent thought suspended.

His arms came around her, moulding her to him— making her vibrantly aware of every hard angle of his body. The kiss deepened, pressuring her lips apart—his

tongue tasting the sweet inner flesh. Kerry found herself
answering in kind, mind and body concentrated on the
evocative demand—nostrils filled with the masculine
scent of him. She could feel her nipples tingling, hard-
ening, pressing against his chest.

When he lowered a hand to seek the shape of her
breast through the covering material she made no protest, wanting his touch everywhere as her flesh quivered
beneath the caressing fingers.

It was only when those same fingers moved again to
start unfastening her blouse that some semblance of san-
ity returned. Enough was enough, she told herself forcefully. She had to stay in control if she wanted to win
this game. She put her hand over his, stilling the movement and doing her best to overcome her pounding
heartbeats and trembling limbs.

'Your mother might come in,' she got out.

To do him credit, he made no attempt to force the
issue, releasing the button he was about to slide through
its slot and settling for a final kiss before releasing her.
If he was feeling any frustration at all he certainly wasn't
showing it.

'I doubt if much would shock her,' he said easily, 'but
you're probably right. This is neither the time nor the
place.' He studied her for a moment, then reached out
an unexpected hand to smooth the tumbled chestnut hair
back from her face, his touch a promise in itself. 'You
still didn't give me an answer re the weekend.'

In for a penny, in for a pound, she thought, shelving
all reservations. 'The party sounds an excellent idea,' she
said. 'I just wasn't too keen on being told where I was
going before I'd even been asked.'

'My apologies for jumping the gun.' He sounded anything but penitent. 'A lack of finesse on my part.'

More a case of taking her acceptance for granted,

Kerry reflected. He wasn't accustomed to being turned down. She hardened heart and mind anew.

'What time?' she asked.

'I'll pick you up at the flat at eight. It's an hour's drive.'

'All right.' She turned back with deliberation to the printer. 'I must finish this before I go.'

'Of course.' From the sound of his voice he was more amused than miffed by the dismissal. 'I'll go and say hello to my mother.'

Kerry steeled herself for some parting caress, but it didn't come. A relief, she told herself staunchly, and knew she was lying. She could still feel the imprint of his lips on hers, still register turbulence at the memory of his hard muscularity when he held her close.

She was going to need every ounce of will-power she possessed to stay objective about this, she acknowledged, but she could do it. She *would* do it. This was one campaign Lee Hartford wasn't going to win!

CHAPTER FOUR

WITH her resolution strengthened even further overnight, Kerry took extra-special care when dressing for the evening, plumping for a figure-fitting garnet-coloured dress she had picked up in a sale and had never yet had occasion to wear. Split up to the knee at one side, it sported a deep V neckline which showed the creamy swell of her breasts.

The solid silver necklet and matching earrings had been a twenty-first birthday present from her parents. She only wore them on special occasions and felt a bit uncomfortable putting them on now in the circumstances, but both dress and occasion called for something better than mere costume jewellery.

With her hair piled on top of her head in a gleaming chestnut coil, and high-heeled sandals to add further stature, she felt reasonably confident of holding her own in any company.

Her appearance brought wholehearted approval from Jane at least. 'You'll knock 'em all dead!' she stated with the generosity of spirit which totally excluded envy from her make-up. 'I'll expect a detailed account so keep your eyes and ears open for any upper-class goings-on.'

'I'll try,' Kerry promised, laughing at the instruction. 'I hope you enjoy your evening, too—when you finally get there. I thought you were meeting this Drew at eight?'

Jane lifted slim shoulders in a gesture designed to imply indifference. 'If he's interested enough he'll wait. I'm still not sure mixing working and personal relationships is a good thing anyway.' She added slyly, 'Something you might think about yourself.'

'It isn't Lee Hartford I work for,' Kerry reminded her, blocking out a momentary temptation to confess the truth.

'It's his house you're working in, which amounts to much the same thing. Quite apart from the fact that you're supposed to be totally agin the man to start with.'

Kerry kept her expression neutral. 'Wasn't it you who told me I shouldn't give so much credence to his media profile?'

'Maybe I was wrong. He certainly hasn't wasted much time where you're concerned.' Jane paused, her hazel eyes speculative. 'That hard to resist, is he?'

The burr of the doorbell forestalled any reply Kerry might have made. Jane moved immediately to answer it, flinging open the door with scant regard for any safety rules, gave the man standing there a swift and succinct scrutiny, then glanced back over her shoulder to mouth a wide-eyed 'Wow' in Kerry's direction, before offering a light-hearted, 'Hi, Lee! I'm Jane.'

'Hello, Jane,' he said, obviously highly diverted by the byplay. 'Am I invited in?'

'Sure.' She stood aside to allow him access, closing the door at his back.

Viewing him, Kerry could understand her friend's reaction. Revealed by the open front of his light overcoat, the stark black and white of his dinner suit gave his dark good looks added impact and brought the all-too-familiar curling sensation in her stomach. A reaction best ignored, she told herself hardily.

'Right on time,' she commented.

'What else?' He ran an appreciative eye over her. 'You look wonderful!'

The compliment brought a sudden warm glow to her

cheeks. Blushing like some schoolgirl! she thought in annoyance, hoping it wasn't noticeable.

'Thanks,' she said. 'I'll just get my coat.'

She took another swift assessing glance in the mirror when she went through to the bedroom, trying to see herself as Lee would see her. The circles he would move in were a piece removed from hers. For all its original cost, she doubted if what she was wearing would begin to compare with what the other women there tonight would have on.

Too bad if it didn't, she thought dismissively, reaching for the silky black fabric coat which did duty for evening wear. She had more important things to think about.

Still wearing his own coat, Lee was perched on the arm of a chair chatting with Jane when she went out. He rose without haste on her appearance.

'Jane tells me she found my cuff-link the other day. I knew I'd lost it but I wasn't sure where.'

'I left it on your desk,' Kerry answered, ignoring the other girl's meaningful expression.

'I didn't see it,' he said easily, 'but, then, I wasn't looking. Ready to go?'

A bit late to back out now, even if she'd wanted to, she thought as they moved to the door. The game was on.

Unable to find parking space outside the flats, Lee had left the car on a side street some short distance away. Kerry chose to walk to it with him rather than wait for him to bring the vehicle to her as he'd suggested, although her clothing was scarcely adequate to keep out the cold. He made no comment when she slid, shivering, into her seat, but switched on the fan at full blast to boost heat through quickly.

'How long have you and Jane been sharing accommodation?' he asked casually as he put the car into motion.

'A couple of years,' she confirmed.

'You wouldn't prefer your own place?'

'I can't afford my own place,' she admitted. 'Not comfortably. Flats don't come cheap, even round here. Anyway, I'd miss the company.'

'There could be advantages.'

Kerry tightened her lips, by no means deaf to the nuances. Other women he knew would all have their own places, of course. Sarah for one.

'I'm quite happy with what I've got,' she said a little shortly.

Lee gave a light shrug. 'That's what counts. You've made it very comfortable between you, I must say. Not so easy, I imagine, when you're stuck to a great extent with what your landlord sees fit to provide in the way of furnishings.'

'No, it wasn't.' Kerry made every attempt to sound relaxed again. 'I think he must be colour blind among other things. The wallpaper clashed with the carpet, and the curtains clashed with both. We had to talk him into letting us redecorate.'

'You did it yourselves?'

'Of course. There's nothing more therapeutic than spending a weekend splashing paint around after a hard working week.' Tongue in cheek, she added, 'You should try it.'

'I'll take your word for it,' he returned on a dry note. 'I prefer to take my therapy flat on my back.'

Kerry gave him a swift glance, taking in the chiselled strength of his jawline. 'I doubt if you spend much time just lying around.'

His mouth slanted. 'You see me as a man of action?'

'All the way. You didn't get where you are by standing back and letting others get ahead of you, for sure.'

'No, I don't suppose I did.' It was Lee's turn to wing a glance, obviously not deaf to nuances himself. 'That isn't necessarily commensurate with ruthlessness.'

'It surely has to mean a certain amount. When you took over that electronics company last year you cut the workforce in half.'

'In order to make it a viable concern—which it is right now. If they'd gone on the way they were going there wouldn't have been any jobs at all. That's what happens when administration outstrips production.'

His tone was level, but the message came across loud and clear: don't criticise what you know nothing about. He had a point, Kerry had to admit.

'Do your parents live far from London?' he asked after a moment or two.

Kerry accepted the change of subject more than readily. She was supposed to be enticing him, not setting his back up, she reminded herself.

'Pretty far,' she said. 'Harrogate.'

'You visit regularly?'

'Every few weeks.'

'Because you feel it's your duty or because you really want to?'

'Because I want to, of course.' Her tone had sharpened again despite herself.

'There's no ''of course'' about it,' he returned equably. 'The fact that they're up there while you're down here hardly suggests a close relationship.'

'Salaries are higher down here.'

'So is the cost of living.'

'I manage well enough—and it's a better social life. Anyway,' she added somewhat defensively, 'they're not against me living my own life.'

'I wasn't suggesting you should move back north. My mother is relying on you.'

Kerry waited a moment before asking the question,

aware of treading on delicate ground. 'Don't you find it a little frustrating having her living in the same house?'

'On the premise that I can't have girlfriends staying the night, you mean?'

'Something like that.'

'I can't see her raising any objection but, as it happens, the question doesn't arise.'

'You prefer to keep your love life away from home?'

Lee's eyes were on the road ahead, his expression difficult to read in the shadow-casting sodium lighting from the streetlamps. 'You could say that. The only woman I'd take to my own bed would be the one I married.'

She said softly, 'I can't imagine you married.'

'Stranger things have happened.' He slanted a glance. 'How about you? Do you intend staying single?'

Kerry kept her tone light. 'Like most people, I'm looking for an ideal.'

'Then you'll probably finish up a bitter old maid.'

'Rather that,' she retorted, 'than a bitter divorcee!'

'What might seem a perfect match to begin with can still end up that way,' Lee returned mildly. 'My parents are a case in point.'

Shooting your mouth off again, Kerry told herself ruefully. 'How old were you when it happened?' she asked after a moment.

He shrugged. 'Fifteen or so.'

'It must have been horrible for you.'

'I was pretty cut up about it at the time,' he admitted, 'but I realised they were better apart than together. My father found it difficult to take a background seat.'

He'd been in that position himself, Kerry reflected. First to the theatre, then to Richard Sullivan. Only when minus both had Estelle turned to her son. It had to be to his credit that he'd offered her a home now.

'Do you see your father at all?' she ventured.

'Occasionally. He's no longer in England.' His tone
briskened. 'Let's find another topic.'

Kerry was only too ready to comply. For a moment
or two she had forgotten why she was here in the first
place. He might have felt some compassion for his
mother, but he'd had none at all for Sarah—or for any
of the others he'd dumped by the wayside either.

All the same he was good company, she was bound
to admit over the course of the journey. It took a conscious effort to keep her prime objective in the forefront
of her mind. No matter how well they appeared to get
along on the surface his interest in her certainly went no
deeper than the obvious. Just another notch he fancied
carving on his gunstock.

They were out in the country, with the headlights revealing a narrow, tree-lined road with little sign of habi-
tation, when he drew up unexpectedly at the roadside.

'I may not have much opportunity to do this once we
get there,' he said purposefully, 'so I'll take it now.'

All part of the technique, Kerry told herself as the
sensually charged mouth claimed hers. And all part of
her plan to have him believe her well and truly capti-
vated by it, she added in defence of her lack of resistance. His hands were around her head, tilting her face
to his—his fingers strong and supple at her nape. She
felt herself drowning in sheer sensation.

When he slid one hand down over her throat to reach
her breast she still raised no protest. The caress was delicate, a feather-light tracery of fingertips over her full
firm shape, brushing bare skin within the V of her dress
and arousing a need for more—for a whole lot more.
She wanted to seize his hand and crush it to her, feel
the warmth and weight of his palm holding her, lifting
her to his lips.

'I want you, Kerry,' he said softly.

At this precise moment she wanted him, too—that

much she couldn't get away from, shame her though it might. 'You can't always have what you want,' she murmured on a husky note—a message meant as much for herself as for him.

'You can if you want it enough.' Dark and fathomless, his eyes searched her face which was still uptilted to his by the pressure of his hand at her nape. 'Challenge is my lifeblood. You presented one the first time I laid eyes on you when you looked at me as if I'd just crawled out from under a stone!'

He paused, as if waiting for some response from her, then gave a low laugh and set her back in her seat, regarding her with mock apology. 'I'm afraid I've messed up your hair.'

'If it comes to that, you have lipstick on your chin,' she said unsteadily. 'Perhaps we should both tidy up before we go any further.'

'Right enough.' He took a handkerchief from his pocket. 'The estate gates are just around the next bend.'

Kerry fished a small comb from her purse and ran it up through the escaping tendrils of hair at her nape, tucking them back in with her fingers, then pulled down the sun visor to renew her lipstick in the vanity mirror. Her eyes looked over-bright in the reflected light from the headlamps still on full beam, her skin warmly flushed. She was aware with every tingling fibre of the man at her side.

I want you, he had said—and I'm going to have you, had been the intimation. Considering the way she had responded to him just now, he could, she supposed, be excused for believing her just about ready to accommodate him.

And, considering the kind of response he did draw from her, she was going to find it increasingly difficult to stay on top of the situation, she acknowledged wryly.

If she wanted to achieve her aim she had better start exercising a little self-control as of now!

Winster Hall lay at the end of a quarter-mile drive through tree-studded parkland. Large, square and brightly lit, it was fronted by a courtyard already filled to overflowing with cars. Lee wasted no time looking for space but followed the drive round and through a stone archway into what appeared to be a stable yard, although the loose boxes to one side had been converted into garages, Kerry saw when she got out of the car.

'We'll go in the back way,' Lee said. 'Those heels of yours aren't made for walking far.'

'They're comfortable enough,' she said defensively. 'I was hardly going to wear hiking boots with this outfit!'

'It wasn't a criticism,' came the dry return. 'You look great. I like you in high heels.'

He would no doubt like them off her, too, she thought cynically—along with everything else! She did her best not to stiffen when he slid an arm about her waist as they trod across the cobbles to a doorway, but was grateful for his solicitude when she stumbled over a jutting edge. Without his supporting arm she would probably have knocked up both knees.

The door gave onto a covered passage connecting with the rear premises of the house. The sound of music drew them along a corridor and into a huge hall from which an imposing staircase rose to an open gallery. A twelve-foot, beautifully decorated Christmas tree occupied a central position, but still left plenty of room for the groups of people standing around with glasses in hand.

Open double doors to either side of the hall revealed yet more people. The hum of voices almost drowned out the music issuing from some unseen source.

Lee addressed the elderly maid who took their coats with the familiarity of long acquaintance, drawing a

smile and a look Kerry recognised only too well. He
radiated machismo to young and not so young alike.

'So let's go find our hosts,' he said, slipping a hand
through her arm to steer her through the throng.

Progress was slow, owing to the greetings coming
from all sides. Lee acknowledged them all, but made no
attempt to pause and join a group.

'Do you know *everyone* here?' Kerry felt moved to
ask.

'Depends what you mean by know,' he said. 'I'm acquainted with most, but I'd only count a few as friends.
Philip's the closest. We go back a long way.'

Just ahead of them an ash-blonde in a sheer black
sheath of a dress broke away from a group to greet him
with an ardour that totally excluded Kerry.

'Lee, darling! I was beginning to think you weren't
coming!'

'The evening has barely got started,' he returned, kissing the cheek presented to him. 'Renata, meet Kerry
Pierson. Philip's wife,' he added for Kerry's benefit.

Kerry put out a hand, conscious of the other woman's
change of expression as she ran an appraising eye over
her. Whilst falling a little short in the designer gown
stakes, it seemed she might rank high enough in looks
and figure to register a certain impact.

Not that Renata had anything to worry about when it
came to feminine beauty. With her lovely, wilful features, tawny eyes and mass of ashen hair, she was the
most eye-catching woman in the room.

She barely touched fingers before turning her attention
back to Lee, her smile designed to captivate. 'There's
someone I want you to meet. Could be a useful contact.'

'Later, maybe,' he responded, with what to Kerry
came across as a total lack of enthusiasm. 'Where's
Phil?'

Looking less than delighted at the deferment, Renata

waved a vague hand. 'Last time I saw him he was with the Glendons—over there somewhere. At least have a drink before you go looking for him.'

'Why not?' Grey eyes turned to Kerry, the sudden hint of devilry obvious to her if not to the other woman. 'What would you like, darling?'

'A gin and tonic, please, darling,' she returned with the same inflection, and saw the gleam increase.

'That shouldn't present any problem. Shall I freshen your glass for you, Renata?'

'I'm fine for the moment, thanks,' came the somewhat short response.

'Then I'll leave you to introduce Kerry to a few people while I go find the bar.'

'The caterers set it up in the library.' Renata looked and sounded more than a little put out. 'Phil refused to have waiter service this time. He says they cause more trouble than they save.'

'Remembering the mess that dropped tray caused last time, he's probably right.'

Kerry resisted the urge to say she would go with him as he started to move off, turning a bright smile on her hostess.

'Please don't feel you have to look after me. You must have a lot of circulating to do.'

The tawny eyes lacked warmth, although her manner was cordial enough. 'Plenty of time. Our affairs never end early. Come and meet some people.'

Moving alongside her towards the group she had recently left, Kerry hoped Lee wasn't planning on staying through to the bitter end. If so, she would be phoning for a taxi to take her back to Battersea, whatever it might cost.

Having performed the introductions, Renata moved on, leaving her to face a clique of total strangers whose interest in her was fired only by the fact that she was here with Lee Hartford. The latest in a long line, she reflected drily.

She was still with the same group when he came back with their drinks. He rested a proprietary arm across her shoulders while exchanging pleasantries with the others, excusing the two of them after a few minutes to go and find their host.

'There's dancing across the hall, if you feel like it later on,' he said as they once more wended a way through the crowd.

Close contact on a crowded floor wasn't going to help her objectivity, Kerry knew, but she could hardly say no. 'Love to,' she agreed. 'I haven't danced in ages!'

'Then Cinderella shall go to the ball!'

'Providing she leaves before midnight,' she quipped.

Lee gave her a swift glance. 'You're not serious?'

'It's a long drive back,' she pointed out.

'And Sunday tomorrow so you can catch up on your sleep, if that's the concern.' He added equably, 'On the other hand, we can always slip away after an hour or so and finish off the evening elsewhere, if you prefer.'

Elsewhere meaning somewhere on their own, she judged, and did a hasty reshuffle. She wasn't ready to tackle any final confrontation as yet.

'I was joking,' she claimed. 'I'm no party-pooper. As you said, it's Sunday tomorrow.'

They found their host chatting with a group on the far side of the room. Tall and slim, with sandy hair brushed back from a boyishly attractive face, he emanated *bonhomie*.

'Where has Lee been hiding *you*?' he asked.

'The cupboard under the stairs,' Kerry answered. 'He only brings me out on special occasions.'

'Humour, too!' He quirked an eyebrow in Lee's direction. 'You hit the jackpot this time, old chum!'

The other man grinned. 'It wasn't easy. Kerry's into self-sufficiency in a big way.'

Philip gave her a further appraisal. 'A feminist?'

'A realist,' she corrected. 'You give a good party, Philip.'

'All down to my wife. Did you get to meet her yet?'

'A few minutes ago,' Kerry confirmed. 'She's very beautiful.'

'I'm a lucky man.' The irony was faint but still unmistakable. 'We're holding a fancy dress ball New Year's Eve. If you'd like to come I'm sure Lee would be only too ready to bring you.'

'Other arrangements, I'm afraid,' said the latter smoothly, drawing a wry grimace.

'Can't say I blame you. Dressing up isn't much to my taste either.'

Then why do it? thought Kerry. He didn't come across as a man to be ruled by wifely whims. She doubted if he and Lee would be such obviously close friends if he were that type.

As if on cue, Renata herself appeared at his elbow, her smile scintillating. 'Lee, the man I told you about is *very* anxious to meet you,' she declared. 'Phil will look after Kerry for you, won't you, darling?'

'Nothing would give me more pleasure,' he said.

This time Lee allowed himself to be usurped, although still displaying little interest in the meeting. There was more to his previous refusal than a simple aversion to being organised, Kerry suspected, watching the two of them depart. She had the distinct impression that he had been giving Renata herself the elbow.

'Would you like to dance?' asked Philip. 'It may be a bit crowded but better than just standing around.'

Kerry brought her attention back to her host, directing a smile and a nod. 'Yes, please.'

It took time to reach the other room for the simple

reason that, unlike Lee, Philip obviously felt it incumbent on him as host to linger a few minutes here and there. He breathed an audible sigh of relief when they finally made it.

The cleared area of floor wasn't as tiny as Kerry had anticipated, although there were certainly plenty of people taking advantage of it. A four-piece group was ensconced in a corner.

By perforce, Philip held her close when they took to the floor, though not in any unduly intimate manner. He was a little shorter than Lee, and of a slighter build, but there was nothing weak about him.

'How long have you two known each other?' he asked as they slowly circled.

'A couple of weeks,' Kerry acknowledged, thinking it seemed a lot longer. 'I'm working for his mother at the moment.'

'You are?' He sounded intrigued. 'In what capacity?'

'Secretary. She's writing her memoirs.'

'That should be interesting.'

'It is.'

'And Lee?' he asked.

She lifted her shoulders, her tone as inconsequential as she could make it. 'Just casual.'

'I'd have said rather more than that—from his side, at least.'

'It takes two to tango,' she rejoined, wincing inwardly at the cliché.

Philip chuckled. 'You're just what he needs, Kerry. A woman capable of keeping him on his toes. It's time he thought about getting hitched.'

Her laugh was forced. 'Not to me, thanks!'

'That makes you even more unusual. There isn't a woman here—married or single—who'd cock a snoot at landing Lee Hartford, given half a chance.'

Including his own wife? Kerry wondered fleetingly. Aloud, she said lightly, 'Are you prone to exaggeration?'

He grinned. 'All right, so let's just say that few of them would give him the brush-off if he showed an interest. He had the same pulling power back in our college days. Used to drive all the other guys green—including yours truly.'

'I doubt if you went short of girlfriends.'

'That's another story.' He looked down at her for a moment in silence, eyes suddenly serious. 'You come across as a whole lot deeper than the general run. You'd be good for him.'

'But would he be good for me?' she countered.

'I'd say so. Lee's straight as they come, no matter what some try to make out. It's the old story—laud effort, vilify success!'

It wasn't his business ethics she had been thinking of, but she refrained from saying so. Whatever else Lee Hartford may or may not be, his reputation as a womaniser was certainly merited. The way he'd come on to her so fast underlined the fact.

And what did the way she had come on to him so fast make her? came the thought, hastily dismissed.

There was still no sign of him when Philip asked if she was ready to eat. She said yes because it was easier rather than from any overriding hunger, but had to confess to a sudden upsurge of appetite on seeing the mouth-watering buffet laid out in the dining hall.

Philip found them a spare sofa through in an anteroom and hitched up an occasional table to take their drinks while they ate, showing no indication at all of being in a hurry to leave her. They were laughing together over a rather risqué but extremely funny story he'd just told when Lee and Renata put in an appearance.

'Are we allowed to share the joke?' asked the latter, looking a little piqued.

'You didn't appreciate it the first time,' answered her husband drily. 'And Lee's already heard it.'

'Oh, one of *those*!' The curl of her lip left no doubt as to the intimation.

Kerry met the disdainful glance steadily, not about to let herself be put down. 'The catering is really superb!'

'I'm glad you're enjoying it so much,' Renata said, with a meaningful look at her plate. 'Personally, I find it impossible to eat at all this late.'

'You don't eat enough to keep a sparrow alive at the best of times,' commented her husband. 'If you're joining us I'll go find a couple of spare chairs.'

'I'll fetch the ones over there across,' proffered Lee before Renata could answer.

Philip stood up with old-fashioned courtesy to offer his wife his seat on the sofa as the other man moved off.

'Lee tells me you're helping his mother write her memoirs,' said Renata on a note of condescension. 'How very interesting for you.'

'I just take dictation,' Kerry answered levelly. 'They're all Estelle's words.'

Finely lined brows lifted. 'You're obviously on very good terms.'

'She doesn't care for formality.'

'It's just what she needs to take her out of herself,' put in Philip, and received a derisive glance from his wife.

'How can writing one's memoirs take one out of oneself? Personally, I don't think raking up the past is ever a good idea.'

'That depends, surely, on the particular past?' said Kerry. 'Some are more interesting than others.'

The tawny eyes swung her way again, the frost chilling. 'Oh, well, there's a job in it for you, of course.'

'A very good one,' Kerry agreed, controlling the urge

to swing a swift kick at the nearest elegant ankle. 'Opportunities like this don't come along very often.'

'I can imagine.'

Lee's return with the chairs brought the subject to an end. Philip looked impassive, although Kerry found it hard to believe him entirely in tune with his wife's attitude. She felt like getting up and leaving the three of them on their own. They inhabited a world she not only had no experience of but didn't find particularly appealing right now.

Having fetched the chairs, Lee made no attempt to take one. 'If you've finished eating,' he said to Kerry, 'how about that dance?'

'I have, and I'd *love* to,' she declared with deliberate extravagance, purely for Renata's benefit.

His expression didn't alter, but the grey eyes glinted in recognition. 'You'll excuse us, Renata—Phil?'

It was Philip who answered, his tone indulgent. 'Have fun, children!'

Lee grinned, taking Kerry's hand as she got to her feet. 'We'll do our best.'

The group was going strong again, having had a half-hour break for food and drink. Reaching the floor, Lee drew her close and put both arms around her. Rather than put her own arms about his neck, she rested her hands flat against his upper chest, easing the tingling pressure on her breasts. She could feel her nipples peaking already to the contact, and knew he would be aware of it, too.

'You smell wonderful,' he murmured, his face close to her hair. 'Georgio, isn't it?'

'Yes.' Her voice sounded suddenly uneven. 'You're obviously an expert.'

'It's one of the more memorable perfumes. You feel wonderful, too,' he added. 'Even more so if you'd relax.

I'm hardly going to do anything too untoward in the middle of a dance floor.'

With the tension building inside her as it was, there was no way she could relax, thought Kerry wryly. Her whole body felt wired, her skin prickling as if ants were crawling under it. She could feel the hard muscles of his thighs as they moved in slow unison, and the radiating heat of him. His heartbeat was strong and regular, unlike her own which was rapidly increasing.

When he kissed her she responded without reservation, turning a deaf ear to the voice of caution. Holding back was hardly going to further the impression that she was finding him harder and harder to resist, she defended herself. She had to build him up to a peak of expectation, before kicking him off the summit.

His mouth was a source of endless pleasure. The silky slide of his tongue between her lips sent tremor after tremor running through her. She answered with mounting sensuality, oblivious to the people about them—oblivious to everything but the moment.

It took the ending of a music session to bring her down to earth. They weren't by any means the only ones on the floor indulging themselves in like manner, but that didn't help her feel anything less of an exhibitionist.

If she wanted to make this campaign of hers last a while she had better start keeping a little more distance between the two of them, she thought ruefully. He undermined all her finer instincts.

'What time is it?' she asked without looking at him directly.

'Just gone twelve thirty,' he answered, glancing at his watch. 'If you're thinking about leaving you'd best forget it. It's snowing a regular blizzard out there.'

CHAPTER FIVE

SNOW hadn't been forecast, was Kerry's first thought. On the other hand, she hadn't heard a forecast today, had she?

'How long since it started?' she asked.

Lee shrugged. 'An hour or so maybe.'

'Then it's hardly going to be very thick yet.'

'On the ground maybe not, but visibility is down to a few yards—or it was.'

'If you knew about it why on earth didn't you say something?' she demanded.

'Because it was already coming down too heavily for safe driving when I found out.'

The music started up again, but Kerry ignored it. 'It can't possibly be that bad!' she exclaimed.

Standing still in the middle of the floor, they were drawing curious glances from those forced to move around them. Lee turned her in front of him, directing her off the dance floor and over to a window—sweeping the heavy curtains aside to reveal a world turned impenetrably white.

With the general clamour going on in here, the rising wind had made little impression, but from the way the snow was driving against the glass it was yet another factor to be reckoned with.

There was no way, Kerry realised, that they were going to get away from the hall tonight. Unless absolutely forced, there was no way anyone should venture outside at all in such weather conditions.

'Satisfied?' he asked.

'I have to be,' she conceded reluctantly. 'If it's still

fine in town Jane is going to wonder what happened, though.'

'You can always phone,' he pointed out.

'She'll probably be in bed and fast asleep by now.'

'First thing in the morning, then.'

'Supposing it keeps on like this?' She took another look out of the window.

'Daylight makes a lot of difference, but we'll just have to wait and see.'

'But all these people…'

'Don't worry about it.' Lee let the drapes fall back into place. 'There are plenty of spare beds, should you feel the need.'

'I'm not particularly tired,' she said, playing dumb.

His smile was a goad in itself. 'In that case, you might like to dance again.'

'What I'd really like is a drink,' she claimed, unwilling to get too close. 'Champagne,' she added recklessly, 'if there's any left.'

'I'll be very surprised if there isn't. The Winster tap never runs dry these days.'

'Phil doesn't seem the partying type,' Kerry commented as they moved away from the window. 'Not on this level, anyway.'

'He isn't. Renata's the party girl. What he really needs is a son and heir but I'd doubt if she has any intention of getting pregnant.'

Kerry somehow doubted it too. Renata and motherhood just didn't go together somehow.

'What do you think he might do if she doesn't give him a child?' she queried curiously.

The reply was dispassionate. 'He has a duty, in his estimation, to continue the Lattimer line.'

'You mean he'll divorce her and marry again?'

'It's possible. Not that Renata would lose out financially.' Lee gave her a slightly narrowed glance. 'Why the interest anyway? I didn't detect much of a rapport between the two of you.'

'That doesn't mean I can't empathise.'

'Wasted on Renata. She can take care of herself.'

He was right about that, Kerry was sure. The woman gave every impression of being totally in control of her life. Lee obviously knew her pretty well—it was even possible that he had known her first. If she'd dropped him to marry Philip it might explain his attitude. He didn't like losing in any sphere.

As forecast, there proved to be no shortage of champagne when they reached the bar. Lee opted for the same himself, claiming dispensation as he wouldn't be driving for several hours. It was going to be a long night, Kerry reflected, feeling the fast-becoming-familiar tingle when his fingers brushed hers when handing her the glass. She would need to keep a steady head in more ways than the one.

What ever the conditions outside, no one else seemed overly concerned. Kerry did her best over the next hour or so to make merry with the rest, but began to find it more and more of an effort.

Lee showed no sign of tiredness. Indefatigable in every sense, she thought sourly, watching him turning on the charm for one of the other women in the group they were a part of at present who was making no secret of *her* proclivities. If he was thinking to arouse her jealousy by showing interest in others he was failing. All she did feel was contempt.

'Refill?' asked the man standing next to her, indicating her almost-empty glass. 'You've been nursing that for the last half-hour.'

Intentionally, Kerry could have told him. She shook her head. 'I've had enough, thanks.'

'I wish my wife knew when *she'd* had enough,' he

remarked drily. 'If she sends out any stronger signals she'll go up in smoke herself!'

Not exactly a one-sided exchange from where she was standing, Kerry thought, seeing the smile flit across Lee's face as he caught the fingers the woman was running coquettishly up his chest. He was giving her every encouragement.

She was tempted to give *him* the cold shoulder when he moved back to her side a little while after, but that would only have suggested that she minded what he got up to.

'Sorry about that,' he murmured. 'Moira tends to get a bit carried away when she's had a few too many. The band's still playing, if you fancy dancing again.'

'Why not?' she said airily, determined not to show any resentment. 'The night's still young!'

She regretted the impulse the moment he took her in his arms. He made no attempt to kiss her this time, just held her close, but her responses were the same. Weak at more than just the knees, she thought wryly, reminding herself of the reason she was doing this. What she needed was backbone.

'You've gone all tense again,' he commented, looking down at her. 'What are you afraid of?'

'Nothing,' she denied. 'I'm just…tired, I suppose.'

Tiredness would be more likely to make her relax, but he let it stand. 'You could always go to bed,' he suggested without particular inflection. 'Renata usually has one or two rooms prepared for those who can't last the distance at these affairs. On your own,' he added, seeing her expression alter. 'If that's what you want?'

Her mind shied away from the question. 'I wouldn't mind getting my head down for a couple of hours.'

'So let's go find you somewhere,' he said.

He made no attempt to look for either Philip or Renata, but made straight for the stairs. Kerry went with

him dubiously, wondering if he was as ready to accept
her tacit rebuff as he made out. If he did try anything
on she had to be ready for him—and not in the way *he*
would have in mind. Definitely not!

The room he selected was halfway along a corridor
running off the open gallery—a spacious room, beautifully furnished and decorated, the curtains already drawn
and the double bed turned back.

'You'd better lock the door so you won't be disturbed
by anyone else seeking rest and recuperation,' Lee advised.

He had come no further than the doorway himself.
Kerry looked back at him uncertainly. His jacket was
open, shirt front still pristine white beneath and trouser
waistband showing no hint of strain. Lithe as a panther,
and twice as dangerous, she thought, feeling her heart
begin an irregular tattoo against the wall of her chest as
she met the all-too-perceptive grey gaze.

She had wanted him earlier, and she wanted him
now—there was no getting away from that. She wanted
to be crushed in those arms of his, to feel his mouth on
hers, his hands caressing her body. Pure lust, and sham-
ing, but she couldn't help it.

When he moved it was with deliberation, coming into
the room and closing the door behind him—turning the
key in the lock with a fateful click. The time to say no
was now, but the word wouldn't come. She just stood
there as he came towards her, her eyes darkened, mouth
dry and heart thudding like a trip-hammer.

'I've been wanting to do this all evening,' he said,
and deftly removed the pins holding up her hair to allow
it to tumble down to her shoulders. He ran his fingers
into the gleaming thickness, beginning a gentle stroking
motion behind her ear lobes as he lifted her face to his.
His eyes had darkened too, except for the small flame

flickering in their depths. She felt tremor after tremor run through her, felt her knees turn to jelly.

Any reservations left at the back of her mind vanished like smoke when he bent his head to kiss her. Her lips parted of their own accord, her tongue touching, twisting, twining with his. Heat began radiating outwards from a central core, making her tremble as it gathered in strength and potency.

She slid her arms about his neck to bring herself closer, pressing her breasts against the hardness of his chest in an almost masochistic craving to be even closer still—thrilling to his strength, his taut muscularity, his whole masculine configuration.

The long zip at the back of her dress slid down easily to his pull. With nothing to hold it, the material fell away from her shoulders, the whole garment dropping the length of her body as Lee eased her just far enough away.

All she had on underneath was a pair of lacy briefs and filmy garter stockings, but she was too far gone to feel any reticence. His hands were cool on her bared breasts yet they lit fires inside her as his fingers encircled her, creating a frenzy of sensation as they explored the full firm curves.

Swinging her up in his arms, he carried her over to the bed and laid her down on top of the covers. The amber-tinted bedside lamps turned her skin golden. He knelt over her and ran his hands slowly down from her breasts to the indentation of her waist, curving them to the shape of her hips with a look in his eyes which left nothing to be desired.

'Beautiful all the way through!' he murmured.

Had she been capable of thinking clearly at all by then, she might have found the speed and dexterity with which Lee shed his clothing only too indicative of the number of times he had played this scene before. His chest was bronzed and deep, the V of dark hair tapering down to the taut ridging of muscle above the waistband of his trousers.

Her own stomach muscles contracted when he stood up to drop the latter and peel them from his feet along with shoes and socks, registering his arousal. Then the dark blue briefs were gone too, and he was coming back to her, shoulders spreading like wings above her as he lowered himself, his mouth seeking hers with a passion that roused her to instant and like response.

In the moments following Kerry lost all sense of time and place. His lips left scarcely any part of her unexplored, igniting a blaze that became an inferno and driving her wild with desire for more—for anything and everything!

When he finally parted her thighs to take him she could hardly wait, her fingers digging into his broad back as they came wholly and wonderfully together, her hips lifting to the long, deep thrusts and her lips parting in a silent scream as they climaxed in almost perfect unison.

The chiming of a clock somewhere brought a reluctant return to consciousness. Dazedly, Kerry counted the strokes, unable to believe the evidence of her ears. *Six* o'clock! The night was over!

Lee stirred at her movement, the arm thrown across her shifting upwards and his hand seeking her breast. She stiffened to his touch, hardly daring to turn her head towards the dark one occupying the pillow at her side. He was still asleep she saw when she finally plucked up the nerve, his face relaxed under hair falling in a thick comma across his forehead and his jawline darkened by the night's growth.

They were lying on top of the covers still, the bedside lamps casting a soft glow. The room was warm, the central heating pump humming softly through the pipes. Apart from that, and the steady rhythm of Lee's breathing, she could hear no sound.

For all her big ideas about teaching this man a lesson, she had succumbed with scarcely a token struggle in the end, she acknowledged painfully. She was no better than he was when it came right down to it. Worse, in fact, because he'd made no secret of his feelings where she was concerned.

I want you, he'd said, and now he'd had her—and not just the once, at that. One of the easiest conquests he'd probably ever made!

She ran her eyes down the lean, fit length of his body, remembering the driving force of those hard-hewn loins. Wonderful while it had lasted—she could hardly deny that—but what was she left with? She had given herself to a man she hardly knew, much less loved, and for no better reason than basic lust. The champagne wasn't to blame. She hadn't had enough of it to undermine reason.

Gingerly she attempted to move his hand away from her, freezing as he murmured something and drew her closer still. The hand moved downwards, coming to rest on the plane of her stomach. Kerry's breath caught in her throat and she waited rigidly for some further movement, aware of the deep-down part of her that wanted it to happen again.

Whatever he might lack in other departments, his love-making left nothing to be desired. She could feel the hunger growing in her, beginning to crowd out other concerns. Having fallen already, why not make a complete gourmand of herself?

It took every ounce of will-power she had left to ease out from under the possessively splayed fingers. Lee opened his eyes as she sat up, coming awake all of a piece—his expression reminiscent as he looked up at her.

'Going somewhere?'

'It's gone six,' she said, resisting the ridiculous urge to cover her breasts with her hands. 'We must have fallen asleep.'

'Hardly surprising.' He held out an inviting hand. 'It's early yet. Come on back.'

'I think we'd better show our faces before someone comes looking for us,' she said unsteadily, doubting if he had further sleep in mind.

'It's unlikely that anyone even noticed we were missing,' came the dry response. He sat up himself, one dark brow lifting sardonically at her involuntary start. 'Why the jumpiness? If you're not in the mood you're not in the mood. I'm not arguing.'

He moved to the edge of the bed, reaching for his discarded clothing. Smoothly tanned, his back showed faint parallel marks where her nails had dug in. Kerry watched in silence as he dressed, wishing she could summon the same equanimity.

It was a bit late for modesty, considering the way they had been together—he knew her as intimately as it was possible to know anyone. All the same, she couldn't contemplate dressing in front of him.

With his shirt and trousers now on and the black tie slung loosely round his neck, Lee went over to the window and drew back the curtains.

'It's stopped snowing,' he announced, 'but it looks pretty thick out there. Phil will probably get a tractor and plough up from the farm come daylight. Till then I'm afraid we're stuck.'

Kerry was past caring. Whenever they got away it wouldn't make any difference to the way she felt about herself. What she had to do was put a good face on things—to act as if last night meant no more to her than it did to him. Whether she could go on working for his mother in the circumstances was another matter.

He turned back to look at her when she made no response, his brows drawing together as he registered her closed expression. 'Something wrong?'

'Nothing that a shower and change of clothing wouldn't put right,' she lied.

'The shower's no problem, and I'm sure Renata would find you something to wear. You're about the same size.'

'I'll manage,' she said. 'After all, everyone's going to be in the same boat. What time does it get light?'

'Not before eight this time of year.' He came back to pick up his jacket from the chair where he had slung it, slipping it on but leaving it unfastened. 'I'm going to borrow Phil's bathroom and a razor,' he said, rubbing a hand over his shadowed jawline. 'If you change your mind about that shower there are three spare bathrooms to go at—one of them right next door.'

Kerry forced a lighter tone. 'I think I'd better. I feel like something the cat dragged in!'

His glance went over her, mouth slanting cynically. 'You look like a woman who's spent the night making passionate love, I'm glad to say. I'd hate to think I'd left *no* impression. See you downstairs in half an hour or so.'

She waited until the door had closed in his wake before making a move, gathering her single undergarment from the floor along with her stockings and dress. There was a mirror on the far wall. She winced inwardly at her reflection. Mascara smudges under her eyes, her hair all over the place and her lips looking puffy.

Anyone who saw her like this would know exactly what she had been doing, she thought wryly, searching for a tissue in her evening bag.

She had been deceiving herself all along, of course. The antagonism had been nothing more than camouflage for the attraction that had hit her the very first time she'd set eyes on Lee. Sarah's suggestion had simply provided an excuse to indulge her own interests—and indulge them she certainly had! She could still hardly credit her weakness.

No amount of soul-searching was going to change anything, she acknowledged wearily, dabbing at the mascara smears. She wasn't the first to lose her head over Lee Hartford; she almost certainly wouldn't be the last. The only thing to do was put it down to experience and learn from it.

She found the bathroom luxuriously appointed and holding everything a guest might find a need for, including a set of new, unwrapped toothbrushes. Kerry used one with gratitude, drying it on a towel and slipping it into her bag. A souvenir of a memorable night, she thought with irony.

Showered, she felt fresher both in body and in spirit. She was able to repair the ravages to a great extent via the compact-sized make-up kit she carried around in her bag, and pinned up her hair again, although she felt more than a little incongruous dressed the way she was. At least she hadn't had to sleep in her clothes the way some of those downstairs would have—if they'd slept at all.

It was almost seven by the time she emerged. There were people moving around downstairs now, though at present the gallery remained empty. Kerry hesitated there, reluctant to descend on her own. The sight of Philip approaching from the far end was something of a relief. He was dressed casually in fawn trousers and yellow sweater, with loafers on his feet.

'Lee's using my bathroom, in case you're wondering where he got to,' he advised. 'He's no more a disposable razor fan than I am.'

From the way he said it he was obviously taking it for granted that the two of them had spent the night together, Kerry realised. Either that, or Lee had told him as much—though she somehow doubted the latter. It was difficult to act blasé about it. Judging from the sudden speculative look in Philip's eyes, she was some way from succeeding.

'How about some breakfast?' he asked.

Food was the last thing Kerry felt like at the moment, but it seemed impolite to say so. 'I wouldn't mind some coffee,' she compromised.

'Oh, I think we can do better than that. Come on down to the kitchen and meet our household treasure.'

'Housekeeper?' she hazarded, accompanying him down the stairs.

'Mrs Franklin never puts in an appearance before eight,' he advised, as if that were only to be expected. 'Cook belongs to the old school. She's been with the family over forty years.'

'Is *she* likely to be up and around at this hour?'

'There'd have to be something seriously wrong for her not to be, considering the circumstances. She'll have rousted out the rest of the staff to help, too.'

He offered a cheery greeting to those occupying chairs and sofas in the vicinity. 'Sorry about the sleeping arrangements, everyone. Coffee will be round in a few minutes, food soon after that. The forecast isn't too good, I'm afraid, but with any luck we'll have you all on the road before it starts up again.'

'You're taking it all so calmly,' commented Kerry in bemusement as they moved on.

He gave an easy shrug. 'One of those things. There was snow forecast, but not to this extent.' He opened a green baize door at the rear of the hall, gesturing her through ahead of him. 'We'll cope.'

Big and well equipped, the kitchen bustled with activity. The aroma of grilling bacon stimulated Kerry's taste buds. Cook was a grey-haired, apron-clad woman in her sixties who answered to the name of Tilly and obviously had complete authority over the other staff

present. Busy as she was, she found time to offer an
affable response to Philip's casual introduction.

'Sit you down there,' she invited, indicating the big
white deal table, 'and have some nice hot coffee while
I fetch you a plate apiece.'

'I couldn't...' Kerry began, breaking off at a shake of
the head from Philip. 'Thank you,' she substituted
weakly.

'I should have warned you,' he said as the cook went
across to the range. 'Tilly believes in a good start to the
day. She despairs of Renata so don't you let me down,
too, or I'll never hear the last of it!'

Kerry laughed and gave in. 'I'll try not to.'

She had reason to doubt her word when she saw the
plates Tilly brought back to them. Bacon and scrambled
egg, tomatoes and kidney, mushrooms and sausage. She
had never in her whole life tackled such a breakfast!
Philip chuckled at her expression.

'Just do your best,' he advised. 'Clear the plate and
you might find yourself with a second helping.'

Large heated salvers were being loaded up with more
food. Destined for the dining room, where everyone
could go and help themselves, said Philip. He tucked
into his own breakfast with an appetite that belied his
lean build.

'Pour Miss Pierson and Lord Lattimer more coffee,
Brenda,' Tilly instructed one of the maids.

Kerry eyed her host with suddenly widened eyes.
'You're a *lord*?'

'Inherited, not earned,' he downgraded himself. 'My
three times great-grandfather was the deserving case.'

So Renata was actually Lady Lattimer, Kerry reflected. That might explain a lot. She said lightly, 'I
never had breakfast with a lord before.'

He regarded her quizzically. 'Does it make a difference?'

'Should it?' she countered.

'Not in the least.'

'Then it won't.'

'You're one on your own, Kerry,' he said, laughing. 'If I were free I'd give Lee a run for his money!'

'Mr Lee!' Tilly was looking to the door, her face beaming. 'There's plenty here for you, too.'

'Like old times, Tilly,' he said easily, coming forward to slide into a chair opposite Kerry's. Grey eyes met green, their expression hard to decipher. With his jaw freshly shaved and his dark hair still damp from the shower, he set her pulses leaping all over again. 'I see you've already been indoctrinated,' he remarked, indicating her loaded plate.

'I don't plan on eating it all,' she said, determined not to show any discomfiture. 'Just enough to keep body and soul together.'

Tilly brought another loaded plate across, obviously in her element. 'It's been a long time since you and the master last did this!' she exclaimed.

'And probably an even longer time before we do it again,' Lee responded. 'Nice to repeat old habits on occasion though. I've never found anyone who can make scrambled egg taste the way yours does, Tilly!'

'Get away with you!' she exclaimed fondly. 'You've been kissing that Blarney Stone again!'

He laughed. 'I don't waste kisses on stones.'

Kerry kept her eyes down, her attention apparently fixed on her plate. She could have done with a little more granite in *her* make-up last night, she thought.

It was becoming light outside by the time they'd all finished eating. Kerry's apology for failing to clear her plate was accepted by Tilly with good grace. She had, she gathered, done rather better than anticipated—certainly a whole lot better than most young women were wont to do these days.

'If I ate like that every morning I'd be huge!' she exclaimed when the three of them left the kitchen.

'You're not on your own,' Philip agreed. 'Gone are the days when the two of us used to tackle that lot on a regular basis when you stayed over, eh, Lee?'

'Regretfully.' Tie still hanging loose and jacket unfastened, the other man looked and sounded at ease. 'We had good times.'

Philip laughed. 'Didn't we, though? Remember that weekend we—?' He broke off, glancing at Kerry. 'Well, maybe not.'

'Don't let me hamper your boyhood reminiscences,' she said drily.

'They'll keep,' said Lee, his tone suddenly shorter. 'I'll go and see if the car starts OK. We might manage to get through with four-wheel drive without waiting for the plough.'

Either way, thought Kerry unhappily as he moved off, it was going to be anything but an easy journey. For her, at any rate.

CHAPTER SIX

RENATA still hadn't put in an appearance when they finally got on their way at half past eight. The snow was deep and crisp, drifted to several feet in parts, the sky blue overhead at present but with a heavy overcast steadily growing from the horizon. More snow on top of this, Kerry reckoned, and they really would be in trouble.

Even with four-wheel drive, the pace was slow. Lee drove with care and concentration, saying little. If it hadn't been for her he would probably have stayed on at Winster, she thought. It was obviously a second home to him, anyway.

'I forgot to phone Jane!' she exclaimed, suddenly recalling.

'Is she likely to worry too much, considering the weather?' he said, without taking his eyes from the road ahead.

'It depends whether she realises how bad it is out here. It's hardly likely to be this deep in town—if there's any there at all.'

'I didn't bring the mobile,' he said, 'but we can keep an eye open for a phone box.'

'I think I'd as soon keep going,' Kerry declared quickly. 'I'd hate to get stuck out here in this temperature!'

Lee winged an ironic glance. 'Nothing to what you've been putting out this last hour or two.'

The comment brought warmth to her cheeks. 'What's that supposed to mean?'

'It means that I went to sleep last night with a volcano

and woke up to an iceberg. I'm still trying to work out why.'

Something he wasn't accustomed to, for certain, Kerry reflected. 'What's over is over,' she said on a surprisingly steady note.

Lee cursed beneath his breath as the car found a hidden ice patch. He brought the vehicle back into line again without touching the brake, as Kerry was sure she would have instinctively done.

'Are one-night stands your usual line?' he asked acerbically.

'No, they're not!' Kerry was too incensed by the implication to maintain the cool front. 'What do you—?'

'Then why start now?' he interjected. 'Last night was good for us both. You wouldn't try denying that?'

It was a moment before she could bring herself to answer. With the memory of last night's love-making etched so clearly on her mind, she could hardly claim to have remained unmoved. She wanted him even now— she couldn't deny that either. What she daren't do was let him know just how much.

'I'm not saying it wasn't,' she got out. 'Just that I don't think it a good idea to go any further.'

'Why?' he queried. 'Give one good reason why we shouldn't carry on from here?'

For as long as it lasted, Kerry thought, fighting the sudden temptation. 'Your mother, for a start,' she said.

'How does she come into it?'

'Well...I work for her.'

'You'd still be working for her.' He paused expectantly. 'You said for a start. What other reason do you have?'

'I just don't think it a good idea,' she repeated, unable to come up with anything else.

Lee pulled in suddenly to the roadside, applying the handbrake before turning to take hold of her by the shoulders and draw her forcefully towards him. The kiss was searing, allowing her no retreat. Not that she tried so very hard in any case. She was past any form of rejection by the time he lifted his head, and he knew it.

'Good idea or not, it's what we both want,' he declared. His expression softened a fraction as he looked into the heavily fringed green eyes. 'You're something of a rarity, Kerry. Most women are out for everything they can get from a man!'

'You'd know, of course,' she said, struggling to contain the conflict going on inside her.

'I've a fair idea.' His tone was dry. 'Anyway, that's not the issue. Do we go on?'

Common sense said no, but common sense wasn't doing the dictating, Kerry acknowledged wryly, unable to summon the strength of mind. Last night had been the most fulfilling experience of her life; just thinking about it brought the blood pounding into her ears.

She lowered her gaze to the region of his mouth, remembering the feel of those firm, wonderfully shaped lips on her body. Foolish or not, denying herself any further contact was beyond her.

'We'll take it as read, shall we?' he said when she failed to make any verbal reply. 'A tacit agreement.' He grimaced suddenly as one or two snowflakes drifted across the windscreen. 'I think we'd better get on while the going's good.'

Kerry stayed silent as he put the car into gear again and eased it out from the roadside, the possibility of more snow the last thing on her mind at that moment. Last night had been a bad enough mistake, but entering into an affair with a man of Lee's ilk was an infinitely worse one. Hadn't Sarah's experience taught her anything?

Except that Sarah had been in love with him, whereas her own feelings were, like his for her, purely physical.

Other people indulged such feelings—why shouldn't she do the same? If nothing else, she would at least know sexual fulfilment.

'Why don't you try and get some sleep?' Lee suggested, concentrating on maintaining contact with the hidden roadway. 'It's going to take quite a while at this pace, I'm afraid.'

Kerry was too stimulated to sleep, but she wasn't about to tell him that. Encased in the fur-lined boots Philip had insisted she borrow in order to get out to the car, her feet felt overheated. She slipped them off, wriggling her toes in the thick pile of the carpet. It had been inevitable that it would happen at some point, of course—a part of her had known it all along. That it had happened so comparatively soon was simply a matter of circumstances. If they hadn't come to this party—if it hadn't snowed...

Now or later, the result would have been the same, though. She might be all sorts of a fool for allowing things to go any further than they already had, but she didn't care, she told herself recklessly. To hell with prudence!

Conditions improved the closer they got to town. Kerry's own road had no more than a sprinkling of snow, already turned grey and mushy by the time they reached it. Lee shook his head when she tentatively invited him in for coffee.

'I'd as soon get out of these things.' He tilted her chin for a long, pulse-racing kiss, the spark in his eyes as he regarded the smooth oval face upturned to his a reflection of the fire he had relit inside her. 'See you tomorrow.'

He very likely had other arrangements already made for tonight, she thought, doing her best to conceal her swift deflation. Agreeing to indulge a mutually satisfying relationship hardly conferred a right to question his movements. If she didn't like the idea that he might be seeing other women she had the option of withdrawing from any further personal involvement.

She went indoors without looking back, thankful when the ground-floor flat door remained closed. The elderly couple who occupied it were none too keen on sharing the building with members of a generation they seemed to regard as all tarred with the same brush to start with.

If they'd seen her dressed the way she was at this hour of the morning, they would probably have felt those beliefs vindicated. They wouldn't, Kerry reflected wryly, be all that wrong in her case either.

Not yet dressed herself, Jane was waiting for her when she got in, her eyes agog with anticipation.

'So how was it?' she asked the moment the door was closed.

Kerry lifted her shoulders, adopting what she fondly hoped was a casual tone. 'The kind of affair you might expect of the aristocracy, I suppose.'

'Aristocracy!'

'Philip Lattimer turns out to be a lord.'

'Married?'

Kerry had to laugh. 'Very much so. And not about to obtain a divorce on my account either.'

Jane wrinkled her nose. 'Back to square one, then.' She changed her tone to add, 'I'm assuming you already had breakfast?'

'Yes, although it seems ages ago now.' Kerry dropped her bag on the nearest chair and started towards the kitchen. 'A cup of coffee wouldn't go amiss. Do you want one too?'

'I'll make it while you go and change,' Jane offered. 'Then we can sit down and you can tell me all about it—if you're not too tired, that is.'

If she went to bed Kerry knew she wouldn't sleep.

On the other hand, she didn't really want to talk either. What she did need was to get out of these clothes. Jane was right there. A change of outfit, a cup of fresh coffee and maybe she could start to get things into perspective.

Jane had the coffee all ready when she emerged from the bedroom warmly and comfortably dressed in leggings and sweater.

'You don't seem all that buoyed up,' the other girl commented frankly, handing her a cup as she took a seat. 'Did Lee neglect you?'

Kerry shook her head, not meeting her friend's eyes. 'Not in the least.'

'The perfect gentleman, then?'

'You could say that.'

'But *would* you?' Jane was serious now, obviously recognising the underlying connotation.

Kerry gave a resigned little sigh. 'If you're asking did I sleep with him the answer is yes. And I already know I need my head examining for doing it.'

'Except that it wasn't your head doing the governing.' There was no censure in the comment. 'I imagine he gave a pretty good account of himself?'

'Naturally.' Kerry was unable to keep the irony at bay. 'If practice makes perfect he could hardly do anything else.'

Jane regarded her thoughtfully. 'Are you seeing him again?'

'I can hardly avoid it.'

'I meant privately.'

'Probably.' Kerry put up a hand to forestall the comment she could hear coming. 'I know what I'm doing.'

'Do you?' Jane's tone was frankly sceptical. 'You were cut up enough over Ray Morton's two-timing.'

'That was different.'

'Only in the sense that you weren't really in love with him—even if you thought you were at the time.'

'I'm not in love with Lee.'

'I'll bet you soon could be, though.'

Kerry shook her head emphatically. 'Not a chance. Anyway, how did your date go?'

Jane accepted the change of subject without rancour, although obviously not convinced. 'Better than I expected. Surprising how different people turn out to be away from work.'

'You'll be seeing each other again, then?'

'He's ringing me later about tonight.' She added quickly, 'I can always cancel if you're going to be left at a loose end.'

'You most certainly won't,' returned Kerry warmly. 'I can entertain myself.'

'Well, if you're sure.'

'Perfectly. There's that new series starting on TV, for one thing. I didn't want to miss that. I'll probably take advantage of an early night, too.'

And spend the greater part of it recalling details from the previous one, came the thought. If she were to be really honest with herself, Jane wasn't entirely wrong. What Lee made her feel went beyond mere physical attraction. It was still a long way from love, though, and she intended it to stay that way.

More snow fell during the night, although the inner city districts escaped the worst of it. Admitted to the house by Mrs Ralston next morning, Kerry was only too glad to feel the comfortable warmth of central heating. The gas fires back at the flat were scarcely adequate to temperatures hovering just above freezing.

Lee, it seemed, had already left. She had anticipated no less, but it still left her feeling let down. Estelle made no mention of the weekend until lunchtime, asking casually how she had enjoyed the party.

'Fine,' Kerry told her, hoping her voice didn't betray anything untoward. 'The first lord I ever met.'

Estelle laughed. 'I find it difficult enough to remember myself.' Her tone altered a little. 'What did you think of Renata?'

'She's an excellent hostess.'

'Oh, none better! Whether she's the right wife for Philip is another matter.'

Kerry said carefully, 'You think the title might have been the main attraction?'

'An irresistible one. Philip should have known better at his age.'

If she'd read the signs correctly the spectacles had already lost their rose-coloured coating, Kerry reflected.

A child might help keep the marriage together, though—as Lee himself had intimated—Renata was hardly mothering material. *They'd* probably have been well suited because she couldn't imagine Lee as a family man either. He might even have wanted to marry the woman himself, only to be thrown over in favour of a title. That would certainly explain his attitude toward her.

Whatever, it had no bearing on her own situation. She could keep on telling herself that she could handle the kind of relationship Lee had proposed, but could she? More to the point, *dare* she?

With the memoirs making good headway both in pace and content, it was taking longer to transcribe the morning's work onto disk.

Kerry tried to keep her full attention on the screen but found her ears tuned to every extraneous sound, although it was difficult to hear very much through the thickness of the study walls and door. She thought she heard someone arrive around four, but her only visitor was Mrs Ralston with the usual tea-tray.

By five, when she finished, she had accepted that Lee

wouldn't be coming. There was every chance that he had had second thoughts himself, she supposed, and was staying out of her way until she got the message. If that did turn out to be the case she was probably well out of it, she assured herself, but there was no conviction in the thought.

When she phoned for the usual taxi and was informed that there would be a forty-five-minute delay, due to a breakdown on the Underground creating an increased demand, she stood irresolute for several seconds trying to work out an alternative.

Buses would be packed at this hour, and she would need to change more than once in order to get within striking distance of the flat. In the circumstances, there was nothing for it but to wait, she concluded. Estelle would be more than ready to pass the time with her. The older woman enjoyed companionship.

Invited to enter when she tapped on the sitting-room door, Kerry was disconcerted to find her employer already with company.

'I'm sorry,' she said quickly. 'I didn't realise you had someone here.'

'Don't go,' said Estelle. 'I'd like you to meet my former agent. Gregory Moore—Kerry Pierson.'

In his fifties, bearded, balding and stylishly dressed, the former was already on his feet, a smile on his lips as he took the hand Kerry held out to him.

'I've been hearing how well the memoirs are going with your encouragement,' he said. 'I'm looking forward to a sneak preview.'

'You'll wait until it's published,' declared Estelle. 'Always providing it proves publishable at all, of course.'

'There's no doubt of it,' Kerry assured her. 'It's already a page-turner.'

'You could make your come-back to coincide with the

publication date,' said Gregory, with an air of continuing a former topic. 'Think of the coverage you'd get!'

Estelle shook her head. 'It's still no deal.'

'So what *are* you going to do with the rest of your life?' he demanded.

'Live it, darling,' came the dry return.

His sigh held exasperation. 'Stubborn as they come!' He turned his attention to Kerry, who was feeling more than a little intrusive. 'Did you ever see her perform?'

'Leave it alone, will you, Greg?' Estelle sounded suddenly weary. 'I appreciate what you're trying to do, but I don't—' She looked round in obvious relief as the door opened again, smiling a welcome at her son. 'Lee, look who's here!'

The older man nodded a wry greeting. 'A wasted effort, I'm afraid.'

Lee lifted his shoulders. 'Worth a try.'

Estelle looked from one to the other with sharpened eyes. 'Are you two in cahoots?'

'If you mean did I know Greg was coming to see you the answer's yes,' said her son. He shifted his gaze to Kerry, appraising with a reminiscent flicker the length of shapely leg revealed by her short black skirt. 'Taxi not turn up?'

'There were none available when I phoned,' she said, hoping no one else had read that look correctly. 'A hold-up on the Underground.'

'That explains the extra traffic on the roads. It's taken me over an hour to get through.'

'In that case, you must wait until things have quietened down,' put in Estelle firmly. 'Lee can run you home after dinner.'

'The taxi's already ordered,' Kerry protested.

'I'll cancel it,' said Lee. 'Mother's right. Better if I take you home later. In the meantime, relax. I'm going up to change.'

Relaxing was furthest from Kerry's mind. He had accepted her presence easily enough and apparently still found her a stimulating sight, but that didn't necessarily mean that he was still of the same mind where their personal affairs were concerned. A battle won was a battle over. She could always pre-empt any backing out on his part by doing it herself, of course. Probably the most sensible move all round.

Gregory took his leave soon afterwards. Aware of a certain preoccupation in her employer's manner, Kerry did her best to make easy conversation. There was no doubt that Gregory's visit had unsettled her. It could even be possible that she was tempted by his inducements. Whatever her thoughts, she was keeping them strictly to herself.

Lee had exchanged his suit for tailored grey trousers and fine-knit white sweater when he joined them again. Kerry found her eyes drawn irresistibly from the well-defined mouth down over broad shoulders and swelling biceps, remembering the strength and power in those arms, the ripple of muscle beneath the skin—the way he looked without clothing of any kind. A man in every sense of the word, and devastating as well.

There was no way, she knew, that she could bring herself to give *him* the elbow. Not while he still had this kind of effect on her. She just didn't have the strength of mind.

It was only when she raised her eyes that she realised he was looking straight back at her, with every indication in the quizzical lift of one dark brow that he knew exactly what she was thinking. Unable to stop the flush she could feel rising in her cheeks, she hastily averted her gaze. Wanting a man was one thing—making it quite so obvious was downright embarrassing.

Dinner was served at eight. Asked afterwards what she had eaten, Kerry would have been unable to say with any accuracy. Once or twice she glanced up to find Lee studying her, though with little to be gleaned from the grey eyes. She could only hope she was achieving the same degree of concealment this time.

If Estelle was aware of anything in the atmosphere she gave no sign of it, though Kerry doubted if she would disapprove, anyway. Her son led his own life his own way—she had already made that clear. If her temporary secretary chose to be drawn into an affair with him, that would be her own lookout.

It was Lee himself who prompted their eventual departure after coffee had been served before the fire. Donning a sheepskin jacket, he insisted on going out first to warm up the car interior while Kerry took her leave of his mother.

'Obviously, you'll be going back home for the holiday,' said Estelle, 'but I'd like to get as much as possible done before it. Would you be willing to wait until Christmas Eve to travel? That would give us another three full days.'

'Of course,' Kerry agreed. 'Mom won't be expecting me before then, in any case.' She gave the older woman a smile, wondering what thoughts that bland expression really concealed. 'See you tomorrow, then. And thanks very much for dinner.'

Lee leaned across to open the car door when he saw her coming. He waited until she had fastened her seat belt before he pulled out from the reserved parking space, his ungloved hand drawing her eyes as it dropped to the gear lever. No automatic transmission with four-wheel drive, of course. Not that he'd probably want it, anyway. In charge all the way, that was Lee Hartford.

'Warm enough?' he asked.

'Fine, thanks,' she said. 'It's good of you to turn out like this.'

Lee gave her a speculative glance. 'I thought we were a little way beyond formality.'

'I wasn't being formal, just grateful,' she answered.

'Even rarer.' The ensuing pause was lengthy. When he spoke again it was on a different note. 'I'd like you to help me entertain some people to dinner tomorrow evening.'

Totally unexpected, the request left her floundering for a moment. 'What kind of people?' she asked uncertainly.

'Executive staff. Annual function. I need someone I can rely on.'

Not to take the invitation for anything more than it was, Kerry assumed, but found herself asking anyway, 'For what exactly?'

'To be a good hostess, and not try to drink the bar dry the way the last one did.' His mouth slanted. 'A last-minute replacement when my original choice came down with flu.'

Sarah had had flu last Christmas, Kerry recalled, and shut off that train of thought abruptly. The last person she needed reminding of at present was Sarah.

'Nothing but orange juice,' she promised, taking the plunge.

He laughed. 'I don't think you need turn teetotal. You might find it more convenient to bring your things with you in the morning and change at the house,' he added. 'Save a lot of to-ing and fro-ing.'

Kerry did a hasty, mind's-eye inventory of her wardrobe. Apart from what she had worn on Saturday, the only thing which was going to be even remotely suitable was the eternal little black dress. Not a patch on Renata's, of course, but the cut was good. Anyway, there would be no time to look for anything else so it would have to do.

'Fine,' she agreed. 'I'll do that.'

They were crossing the bridge already, the road sur-

face ahead glinting with frost. By this time on Friday
she would be miles away in Yorkshire, she realised with
a sudden sinking feeling. For a moment she contemplated not going home at all this Christmas, but only for
a moment. She couldn't disappoint her parents. Not for
such utterly selfish reasons. In any case, Lee would no
doubt have plans already made.

'I suppose you'll be joining your family for
Christmas?' he said, as if reading her thoughts. 'Do you
plan on staying through New Year too?'

'I'm not sure,' she replied cautiously. 'It will depend
on when your mother plans to start work again.'

'I don't see her doing it Christmas week—though who
knows? She's never been all that predictable.'

Like mother, like son, Kerry reflected. In some respects, at any rate. Aloud she said, 'Was it your idea to
have her agent make that call this afternoon?'

The shrug was brief. 'More of a mutual effort. It's
what she needs.'

'But not what she seems to want.'

'Not what she's ready to admit, you mean. She's
afraid of being less than she was.'

'That's understandable.'

'It's gutless.' His tone was dispassionate. 'I'd hoped
the biography might give her a kick-start.'

There was still time, thought Kerry. They weren't
even halfway through yet.

Both front bedroom and sitting room lights were on
at the flat, the curtains cosily drawn. Lee declined to
come in on the grounds that he wasn't in the mood for
small talk.

What he was in the mood for was obvious when he
kissed her. For the first time Kerry regretted not having
a place of her own. The way things were, it was going
to be difficult finding anywhere to be together at all.

Something she hadn't thought about before, and doubted if he had either.

'I don't think this is going to work,' she said huskily. 'Circumstances are against it.'

'Circumstances can be altered,' he returned. He seemed about to add something else, then apparently thought better of it, lifting his shoulders in a philosophical shrug. 'Seems we'll just have to exercise patience for the time being. I could be late getting back tomorrow, but we shan't be leaving before eight.'

She didn't want him to leave now. Looking at him, his face lean and dark above the creamy sheepskin, she was swamped by desire. What he'd meant by altering the circumstances she wasn't sure; right this moment she would have settled for anything he suggested, just to be with him a little longer. It took everything she had to keep her voice from reflecting her thoughts.

'I'll be ready whenever,' she promised, and saw his mouth widen fleetingly.

'I'll hold you to that.'

He saw her indoors, before driving off. Standing in the hall and listening to the diminishing engine noise, Kerry wondered if he could possibly be feeling as deprived as she was right now. It was more than just a physical deprivation on her side, if she were honest with herself—which would make her even more of an idiot to get any more deeply involved than she already was.

Lee wanted her for one thing and one thing only. Once surfeited, his appetite would soon die. How would she feel then?

Like hell, came the answer, but it made little difference. Where Lee was concerned she had no will-power left at all.

CHAPTER SEVEN

ALREADY advised of the arrangement, Estelle suggested that the dress Kerry planned to wear for the evening be hung ready in the bedroom she would be using to change in later.

'It has an *en suite* bathroom so you'll be quite private,' she added.

'This was Lee's idea,' Kerry hastened to tell her, not wanting to be thought presumptuous.

'I imagine it was. A good one, too. It saves a lot of trouble.' The other rested a shrewd gaze on Kerry. 'If there's any doubt left I've nothing whatsoever against you and Lee getting together. I'd have been surprised if he'd failed to show an interest.'

There was a brief hesitation before she added tentatively, 'I'm probably speaking out of turn, but don't take things too seriously. He's my son, but that doesn't mean I'm blind to his faults. Constancy isn't exactly one of his virtues. Not where women are concerned, at any rate.'

Kerry kept her tone level, her emotions under firm control. 'That's all right. I'm no more looking for a husband than Lee is for a wife. And I think we ought to get started,' she added. 'It's going to be lunchtime before we know it.'

Apparently reassured, Estelle settled down to work with a will. Kerry concentrated her attention, clamping down on any inclination toward despondency. Her employer had told her nothing she didn't already know so what was there to consider? She would deal with whatever was to come as and when necessary.

For the first time, Estelle elected to continue dictating after lunch. Her output was increasing, her retrieval excellent. Kerry found it all thoroughly entertaining.

'You know, it wasn't such a bad idea your agent had last night,' she said casually, after reading back one particular passage concerning an appearance in Coward's *Private Lives*. 'I know he already has a part lined up for you.'

'What he can't guarantee is a capacity audience to go with it,' was the somewhat brusque reply. 'I'm not prepared to play to anything less. *You* won't change my mind either so don't waste your time.'

Kerry took her at her word, although deploring the resolution. Estelle still had it in her, she was sure, to regain her theatrical throne.

There was still no sign of Lee when Kerry went up to one of the guest bathrooms to prepare for the evening. Showered and scented, she applied light make-up, blending muted green shadow over her lids and using an eyeliner to give added emphasis.

Scooped at the neckline, the black dress threw her skin into creamy relief. The long tight sleeves and figure-skimming cut were classy—cost wasn't always the criterion. Remembering Lee's preferences, she left her hair loose—defending herself with the thought that she was only doing what thousands of other women did in pandering to a man's tastes.

'Lee got in about twenty minutes ago,' advised Estelle when she went downstairs. 'You look superb!' she added extravagantly. 'Lucky man!'

'Lucky me, too,' Kerry responded lightly. 'It isn't so often I go anywhere worth dressing up for.'

Lee put in an appearance some minutes later, heart-jerking as ever in the black and white. Kerry felt herself melting inside just looking at him, her senses fusing at the memories evoked. She could only hope that the feelings he aroused in her weren't written all over her face.

'You're ravishing,' he declared out in the hall as he helped her on with her coat. 'You'll have all the wives turning green!'

'Not a very flattering colour,' she laughed, warmed by the compliment even while recognising its glibness. 'How many people will be there?'

'A round dozen, including the two of us. Executives only, as I said. The lower ranks have their revelry New Year's Eve by common choice.'

'Is that the prior engagement you told Philip about?' Kerry hazarded.

'Partly. I usually put in an appearance at some point.'

'On your own?'

His mouth widened. 'Would you expect it?'

'Silly question.' She took care to keep her tone inconsequential.

Lee opened the door to let in a blast of cold air, taking her arm as they descended the stone steps to the car then waiting to see her comfortably seated before going round to take his own seat. The courtesies came so naturally to him, she thought. Such a change from the more general attitude.

She slanted a glance at him as they pulled out from the kerb, her pulses leaping once more to the sheer impact of that chiselled profile. They were together for the next few hours at least. Beyond that she didn't intend to think.

The hotel was all decked out for Christmas. They were the last of their party to arrive at the top-floor restaurant with its wide, undraped windows and panoramic views. Approaching the table, Kerry felt the cynosure of all eyes. She fixed a smile on her face as Lee introduced her, knowing she was going to have difficulty tying the various names to the right faces all evening.

On the whole, they seemed a friendly enough crowd. Apart from one other, the men could all give Lee several years apiece, she judged. The only stranger at the table, in addition to being the only woman under thirty, she felt somewhat disadvantaged, although every effort was made to include her in conversation.

When she thought about it the whole situation still seemed a little unreal. A bare month ago she had only known of Lee's existence through the media—now here she was playing hostess for him. Watching him as he talked with Barry Wayland, the chief accountant, and hearing his deep-throated laugh at some shared joke, she longed to be alone with him.

'You're doing me proud,' he said when they finally danced together after he had done his duty by the other women. 'I couldn't have asked for better.'

'I'm enjoying it,' Kerry assured him, lying through her teeth. 'You seem a close-knit team.'

'We share a common aim.' He drew her closer, his hands warm at her back. 'It seems an age since I held you like this.'

It did to her, too, but it was worth the wait to be close again now. She nestled closer still, feeling his breath stirring the hair at her temple. There was no point in playing things cool. Not when their whole relationship was based on a physical desire already recognised and acted upon. It was coming up to midnight. A little less than seventy hours ago they had been in bed together.

'I feel like abandoning this lot and going off somewhere on our own,' Lee growled softly, as if sensing her thoughts.

'Duty takes priority,' she returned, equally softly, wondering where he might have in mind.

'Unfortunately that's true. This particular one, at any rate.' He put his lips to her temple, brushing aside the tendrils of hair and sending a frisson rippling down her spine 'I m going to miss you next week.'

So ask me to stay, she thought recklessly, and immediately felt ashamed. The last thing her mother had said when she'd phoned home as usual on Sunday was how much they were looking forward to seeing her over the holiday. Even if Lee did suggest she stayed on in town she couldn't do it to them. They merited better than that. He'd hardly be spending the time alone, anyway.

'I dare say I'll miss you, too,' she said, quashing any tendency towards possessiveness. She had no special claim on him—any more than he had on her. 'Still, I'm sure we'll both get by.'

'Without a doubt,' he agreed on a dry note. 'I suppose you have friends still up there?'

'Most have done what I did and moved away, but they'll be going home for Christmas, I expect. It's a special time: a family time. Worth making an effort for.'

'Where there's a family to get together, I'm sure you're right.'

Kerry was silent for a moment, trying to evaluate his mood. He had sounded dispassionate enough about it, but was he really? His father was out of the country, he had said on Saturday night, and there appeared to be no other close relatives. Before Estelle had come to live with him he would have been alone in the house but for Mrs Ralston, who could hardly be called the most scintillating company.

'Shall you and your mother be spending Christmas day together?' she asked tentatively.

'I've spent Christmas at Winster for years,' he said. 'She'll be joining us this year.'

'I was under the impression that she doesn't care too much for Renata.'

'There's no great love lost on either side, but they're

both of them capable of putting a good face on things. Anyway, there'll be others there, too.'

Others there or not, the idea of his spending Christmas anywhere near the lovely Renata was unpalatable. Whatever his feelings toward her, she was certainly still interested in him. One of those women who wanted her bread buttered on both sides. Capable of getting it, too, no doubt—although Lee would surely draw the line at betraying his oldest friend.

'Did you decide yet how long you'll be staying up north?' he queried, breaking in on her thoughts.

'Estelle wants to leave the first couple of days in January free to catch up on things,' she said, 'so I suppose I could stay until the second.'

If she was hoping for some contention on his part she was to be disappointed. 'Your parents will be happy about that,' was his only comment.

They would indeed, Kerry agreed disconsolately. She was going to be the one for whom the time passed slowly. Lee was obviously quite content to put everything on hold for a week or more.

A self-possessed brunette in her early thirties, Louise Wayland had had little to say to her during the course of the evening. Finding Kerry renewing her lipstick on her own in the ladies' cloakroom, the older woman more than made up for the omission.

'You might think me an interfering busybody,' she said frankly, 'but it would be wise not to take Lee's attentions too much to heart.'

Kerry looked at her in the mirror, her hand stayed in its action, green eyes frosty. While she was prepared to take similar advice from Estelle, she was damned if she would take it from anyone else!

'I'm not sure what that's supposed to mean,' she said.

'It means that he brings a different partner to this and similar functions every time. Since Renata Scholfield married Philip Lattimer he's been playing the field even more. I believe from what was said earlier that you've already met her?'

Kerry controlled both voice and expression. 'Yes, I have.'

'Lee could offer her everything except the title. Renata being Renata, she couldn't resist that. He and Philip being so close made it all the worse, of course. Not that a minor thing like a wedding ring is likely to worry Renata. What she wants she makes sure she gets!'

Kerry studied the other woman's reflection. Obviously no friend of Renata's so hardly a reliable character witness, but her input confirmed what Kerry had suspected regarding Lee's prior involvement with the woman in question. With 'prior' being the operative word, she stressed to herself.

'It's really no concern of mine,' she said steadily.

Louise gave her a bland little smile. 'I just thought you should know, that's all.'

More bitchiness than solicitude, Kerry opined, concentrating on the mirror as the other woman left. Her hand shook a little, smearing the pink outside her lipline. She took a tissue from the holder and corrected the mistake, forcing herself to look at the whole thing rationally.

What difference did it make if Lee *had* asked Renata to marry him at some point? She, herself, was under no misconceptions regarding her own status in his life. If the limitations bothered her she was at liberty to withdraw from the arrangement.

She was in command of herself, outwardly at least, when she left the cloakroom. Lee was talking with Barry again but he slanted a smile at her as she took her seat. Aware of Louise's eyes on her, too, Kerry returned the smile, saw the grey eyes narrow a fraction and realised that her act was by no means perfect. She didn't look at Louise.

The party finally broke up around one-thirty. It was business as usual the following day, Kerry gathered, thinking it would have made more sense to hold the event over until the Thursday evening with Christmas Eve likely to be a slacker day all round.

'Not exactly a riveting event for you, I'm afraid,' said Lee when they were in the car. 'The problem with these affairs is trying to keep business matters from intruding. Sorry if you felt neglected.'

'I didn't feel in the least neglected,' she denied. 'Or bored either. I hope I didn't give that impression.'

'Not initially. You just seemed to withdraw somehow the last hour or so.' He paused, before adding levelly, 'What did Louise say to you earlier?'

'Louise?' Kerry made a pretence of searching her memory. 'I'm not sure which one—'

'Barry Wayland's wife. She followed you to the cloakroom.'

Kerry wrinkled her brow again. 'We were there at the same time but we didn't really make conversation. Why?'

His shrug made light of the matter. 'Just a thought. Louise has a bitchy streak.'

Maybe with some cause where he was concerned, came the thought. Marriage didn't necessarily exclude her from the club. The depression which had been hovering all evening took on new weight. What kind of an idiot was she, she asked herself hollowly, to get mixed up with the likes of Lee Hartford at all? Whatever dubious pleasure she gained from the association it would have to be paid for in the end.

'Not too tired, I hope?' he said softly as she leaned her head back against the rest and closed her eyes.

'For what?' she asked tonelessly. 'Jane will be home.'

'There's always the apartment.'

Her heart gave a painful thud, her head coming sharply upright again. 'What apartment?'

'One we keep for people staying over on business. There's nobody there at present.'

'How would we get in?' was all she could think of to say.

'The hall porter has access to a key.'

It wouldn't be the first time he had taken someone there with him, Kerry guessed, reading between the lines. Better than a hotel room, maybe, but still lending a certain sordidness to the suggestion. She felt a sudden fierce rejection of the whole idea.

'I don't think so,' she said as evenly as she could.

'Your choice.' If he was annoyed at the turn-down he wasn't revealing it. 'Home, then.'

'I'm sorry.' The apology was dragged from her against her will. 'I just don't—'

'I said it was your choice.' This time there was a definite edge to his voice. 'I'm not into persuasion.'

He wouldn't normally need to be, Kerry was sure. If he decided to call time on the whole thing here and now she could hardly complain. He'd made his interests plain enough from the start.

More than half anticipating a swift leave-taking on reaching the flat, she was both surprised and, despite herself, relieved when he switched off the engine and drew her into his arms. If anything, the degree of passion in his kiss was even more pronounced, his hand possessive as he slid it inside the silky black coat to seek soft, warm flesh.

'You have the loveliest breasts,' he murmured against her lips. 'A lovely body altogether! I keep seeing you the way you were Saturday night—feeling you under me so supple and responsive. I've spent the whole damned evening thinking about it. If you're playing me up...'

'I'm not,' she whispered as he let the words trail

away, her mind closed to everything but the feel of those caressing fingers. 'I just didn't fancy facing knowing looks from some hall porter, that's all.'

To do him credit, he didn't attempt to pretend not to understand what she was getting at. Pushing aside the covering material, he bent his head hungrily to take her tingling nipple between his teeth. He lapped it with his tongue until she could barely stand the sensation, his free hand sliding along the length of her leg.

'You're driving me crazy!' he muttered. 'So cool and composed on the surface—so full of fire underneath! If you don't like the idea of the apartment how about moving into the house while you're working on the book? There's plenty of room and it would save you from the morning rush.'

Handy all round, in fact, she thought with irony. 'And have your mother catch you creeping along the landing,' she said.

'What if she did? She's far from being shocked about such matters.'

'Maybe so, but I'd still feel uncomfortable.'

Lee left off what he was doing, removing the hand from her leg to cover her up again with sudden and chilling abruptness.

'So what *would* you go along with?' he asked flatly, sitting back in his seat.

Kerry swallowed on the dryness in her throat. No illusions, she reminded herself.

'I don't know,' she admitted, and steeled herself to go on. 'Perhaps we'd best call it a day and have done.'

The nearest streetlamp was too far away to reveal the expression in the grey eyes. He didn't move yet something in him seemed to harden.

'Is that what you want?'

From somewhere she found the ability to lift her shoulders in a resigned little shrug. 'There doesn't seem to be much point in carrying on, does there? If I had a place of my own it might be different, but—'

The hardness increased. 'Are you suggesting I might set you up in one?'

'No, I'm not!' The sudden searing anger overrode all other considerations. 'If that's what you think then to hell with it all!'

Lee didn't try to stop her as she fumbled blindly for the doorhandle, nor did he get out of the car. Kerry refrained with an effort from slamming the door on him, moving away without a backward glance.

Only when she was safely inside did she come to a halt, leaning her head against the coolness of the lobby wall for a moment in dumb acceptance. So that was that. Over and done. Probably for the best in the long run, anyway.

The problem being that she still had the job to complete, came the reminder. While she couldn't see Lee caring enough to ban her from the house altogether, it was going to be difficult to carry on as if nothing had happened between them. Yet what was the alternative? She couldn't let Estelle down now. Not when the book was going so well.

There had been no lights showing in the sitting-room windows, which meant that Jane was either still out herself or already in bed. Whichever, Kerry told herself wearily as she made her way upstairs, it wasn't her friend's problem.

If Estelle had any notion at all that her son and her secretary were no longer in harmony she was keeping her own counsel on the subject. The morning was exceptionally productive. Kerry was able to lose herself in the wealth of detail to be transcribed on screen in the afternoon.

Lee still hadn't put in an appearance when she departed at five, which was something of a relief. She had already decided to take the evening train tomorrow, rather than tangle with the last-minute rush the following day. With any luck, she thought in the taxi going home, she wouldn't have to face Lee at all.

By the time she returned in the New Year there was every chance that the situation would have resolved itself. What she had to be thankful for was that, unlike Sarah, she was getting out relatively unscathed.

Was she? asked a small voice at the back of her mind, hastily smothered.

The following day passed like any other. Estelle was still on fine form and reluctant to take a lengthy break.

'I'll have lost impetus by the time we get started again,' she complained when the time came to close the chapter. 'I should have waited till after New Year.'

Kerry had thought that initially, but she refrained from saying so.

'You'll soon pick it up again,' she offered comfortingly instead. 'You can jot things down longhand between times just to keep it ticking over.'

'I suppose so.' Estelle sounded far from convinced. 'What time is your train?'

'Six-thirty from King's Cross. I brought my suitcase with me so I could go straight from here.'

'You've time for a snack before you go, then.'

'We only had tea an hour ago,' Kerry reminded her. 'I'll have something when I get in.'

'That can't possibly be before ten o'clock, and there may not even be a buffet car on the train.'

And the longer she lingered the more chance there was of running into Lee, Kerry thought, and took a firm stance.

'I couldn't eat anything else right now, thanks all the

same. Anyway, I'd rather get to the station early than risk missing the train. I've pre-booked a seat.'

Estelle gave in with good grace. 'Very sensible of you. I imagine it's going to be quite hectic.'

'Not nearly as much as it will be tomorrow.' On impulse, Kerry went over to press a swift, light kiss on her employer's cheek. 'Happy Christmas—and thanks again for the present.'

'The same to you, dear,' said the other, returning the gesture. 'And, remember, no peeping before Christmas morning.'

Kerry laughed. 'Definitely not.'

She was ready and waiting in the hall when the taxi she had ordered for five-thirty drew up out front. Three minutes early, she noted by her watch, which was all to the good.

Lifting her case, she went to open the door—her heart performing a painful double beat when she saw Lee mounting the steps. Wearing a short camel overcoat over his suit and with briefcase in hand, he looked businesslike in every sense of the word.

'I was hoping I'd catch you,' he said. 'I'll drive you to the station.'

'The taxi's already here,' Kerry pointed out as the black cab drew up beyond his parked car.

Lee turned back down the steps, taking his wallet from the inside pocket of his jacket as he went. Kerry stood there impotently watching the cab pull away again after he handed over a banknote.

'I'll put your case in the boot,' he said, coming back. 'How much time do we have?'

'An hour.' She hardly knew what to think about this last-minute gesture. 'You didn't need to do this.'

'Yes, I did,' he returned. 'I cut a meeting to be here.'

'I'm flattered.'

He inclined his head, obviously not about to be drawn by her sarcasm. 'So you should be. Are you coming?'

She had, Kerry conceded, little choice. Caution, she warned herself, accompanying him to the car. This might be no more than a parting gesture.

The heavy traffic called for concentration. Lee made no effort to converse during the journey, nor was it possible to tell from his face what he might be thinking. It was ten past six when they reached the station, a quarter past by the time he had parked the car.

Her train was already in. Disregarding her protestations, he secured a platform ticket and carried her suitcase on board to find her seat.

His lip curled in disgust at the sight of the crowded carriage, with tables still bearing debris from the previous journey.

'You can't travel in this!' he declared.

Kerry lifted her shoulders. 'I have a seat. That's more than a lot of others have.'

His lips firmed. Taking her arm, he urged her ahead of him towards the front of the train. There were seats to spare in the first-class carriages, although not that many. Lee lifted her case into an overhead rack.

'Give me your ticket,' he said. 'I'll get it altered.'

'There isn't time,' Kerry protested. 'It's almost half past now. I was fine where I was.'

Taking out his wallet again, he extracted several notes and pressed them into her hand. 'Pay the difference.'

People nearby were taking too great an interest. Reluctantly Kerry took the line of least resistance.

'I'll settle up with you when I get back,' she said with deliberation.

The grey eyes acquired a sudden spark. 'I'll be waiting. Come and see me off.'

She accompanied him from the carriage to the platform door, forcing herself not to overreact when he drew her up to him. His mouth was demanding, eliciting a response she couldn't withhold.

'That's better,' he said. He studied her face with narrowed concentration, as if committing it to memory. 'It isn't over, Kerry. Not by a long way.' Taking a slim, wrapped parcel from his overcoat pocket, he folded her fingers about it. 'Not to be opened until the proper time.'

He was out of the door before she could reply, lifting a hand in farewell as the train began to move. Kerry made some kind of gesture in return, trying not to let this last-minute reconciliation mean too much. The last glimpse she had of him was of a tall, broad-shouldered figure, striding away down the platform. He hadn't even waited until she was out of sight.

CHAPTER EIGHT

VIEWED from her bedroom window, the snow-covered hills and frost-sparkled trees created a Christmas spirit all of their own. A scenic feast, winter and summer alike, Kerry acknowledged, turning back to the cosy warmth. There were times when she dearly missed the sweeping grandeur of the Dales.

Obeying Lee's injunction, she had left the package he had given her unopened, but hadn't put it beneath the tree with the other gifts. Taking it from her bedside drawer now, she stripped off the stylish black and gold paper to reveal a long slim jeweller's case in dark blue leather, which she sat looking at for several uncertain seconds before finally opening it up.

Lying there, so slender and elegant in its white gold casing, the watch took her breath away. It hardly needed the Asprey label to tell her its likely worth. She couldn't accept this, she thought, tight-lipped. It was too much like being bought!

Without attempting to remove the watch from the case, she wrapped it up again and thrust it back into the drawer. The shop would take it back. Lee was probably one of their best customers. In the meantime, it would be safe enough where it was.

Wearing navy-blue leggings and a pale blue lambs-wool tunic, she went downstairs to finish clearing away the remnants of last night's family get-together. She had the table laid for breakfast and bacon sizzling under the grill by the time her mother put in an appearance.

'Your father's tired and having a lie-in,' she announced. 'A little too much festive spirit last night, if you ask me,' she added without rancour. 'I'm glad I don't have to think about cooking lunch myself this year.'

It was a long-standing tradition that Kerry's mother and her mother's two sisters took it in turns to prepare Christmas Day lunch for the whole family. It usually turned out to be a pretty riotous assembly. Last year Kerry had found the occasion exhausting. Her mother wasn't the only one who welcomed the respite.

'I thought we might make the ten o'clock service,' Kerry said, breaking eggs into a bowl for scrambling.

'We might—your father certainly won't.' Ann Pierson tied an apron about her still-slim figure, before taking up the tongs to turn the bacon. 'We'll go straight on to Mary's from church and he can meet us there. Always providing he's feeling up to it by then. He should stay off the whisky. He's just not used to it.'

'He only had two,' remarked Kerry amusedly. 'Hardly a bender. It's just possible that he really is tired. He spent most of yesterday afternoon sawing logs for the fire.'

'You're looking a little bit peaked yourself, if it comes to that,' her mother commented, glancing her way. 'Not coming down with anything, are you?'

'I'm fine,' Kerry assured her.

Ann took her word for it. 'I never got round to asking you yesterday but how's the book doing?'

'That's fine, too, so far as it's got. There's still quite a long way to go before it's finished.'

'I should think you're pleased about that, aren't you? I mean, working in that lovely house—and with some-one as famous as Estelle Lester!' The pause was brief but telling. 'You haven't had a great deal to say about this son of hers. Don't you see much of him?'

'He's out at work most of the time,' Kerry confirmed, her attention on the eggs she was stirring over the heat.

'But you've obviously met him,' her mother insisted. 'What's he really like?'

'He's...OK, I suppose.'

'Is that all?'

Kerry lifted her shoulders in feigned nonchalance, wishing the inquisition would stop. 'What else do you want me to say?'

'Well, I thought—' Ann broke off at the ringing of the telephone, reaching out an arm for the extension placed conveniently close. 'Hello?'

Wondering who would be phoning at eight o'clock Christmas morning, Kerry heard her say, 'Yes, it is. And the same to you, too.' There was a slight pause, a sudden change of tone. 'Kerry? Yes, she's right here. I'll put her on.'

She held out the receiver, her expression a study in curiosity. 'It's Lee Hartford.'

Her heart missing a beat, Kerry put the eggs aside and went to take the instrument. Her voice sounded totally unlike her own. 'Hello?'

'I just called to say Merry Christmas,' said Lee, as clearly as if he were in the same room.

'You already did,' she responded, and heard his low laugh

'So I'm saying it again. Do you like the watch?'

'It's beautiful,' she acknowledged woodenly. 'I can't accept it, of course, but I appreciate the thought.'

'What do you mean, you can't accept it?' he asked on an odd note.

'It's...too much.'

'You mean it's ostentatious?'

'No, of course not. As I said, it's beautiful.' She paused, aware of her mother's wide-eyed interest. 'Can we discuss it when I get back?'

'I'd rather discuss it now.' His tone had hardened a

little. 'What do you think it is—payment for services rendered?'

Kerry winced, unable to deny that the thought had crossed her mind. 'I wouldn't put it quite like that,' she got out.

'But not far from it.' It was Lee's turn to pause. When he spoke again it was on a steadier note. 'I think you're right—we can't sort this out over the phone.'

Kerry replaced the receiver with nerveless fingers as the line went dead. She had made a complete mess of that, she thought hollowly. Not that she regretted turning down the gift.

'So, what was all that about?' asked her mother. 'One minute you're trying to make out you hardly have anything at all to do with Lee Hartford—the next he's ringing up here, desperate to speak to you!'

Kerry managed a weak laugh. 'Don't exaggerate.'

'Who's exaggerating? A man doesn't go to all that trouble just to say a polite hallo to his mother's secretary.'

'We've been out together a time or two,' Kerry fudged. 'Nothing serious.'

'Serious enough for him to give you an expensive Christmas present, from the sound of it.'

'Not the way I see it.'

'So how do you see it?'

'A passing fancy on his part. Which is why I don't intend getting involved to the extent of accepting expensive presents from him.' She forged a smile. 'So let's forget about it, shall we?'

Saying it was one thing and doing it quite another but, with a large and not by any means quiet family around most of the time, Christmas Day and Boxing Day both went by quickly enough.

It was after that, with several days to go before New Year, that time began to drag. Kerry looked up a few old girlfriends but found them either very much married and interested only in houses and babies or settled with boyfriends and a view to the same. In a lot of ways she envied them their contentment.

Fed up by the Thursday, she donned boots and padded anorak and took a neighbour's German shepherd out for a long walk after lunch, invigorated by the crisp, cold air into going even further than she had intended.

It was already getting dark when she finally made it back, the streetlamps welcoming beacons along the road. The sight of the car standing outside the house slowed her footsteps almost to a halt. It couldn't be! she told herself disbelievingly.

Lee got out of the car when he saw her coming, the sheepskin jacket emphasising his breadth of shoulder and the darkness of his hair. The dog at her side started to growl as he moved to intercept him. Kerry quietened the animal with a soft word of reassurance totally at odds with her hammering heartbeat.

'What on earth are you doing here?' she asked, hoping she sounded more composed than she felt.

'What do you think?' came the dry return. 'I could hardly say I was just passing. I've been sitting here for the last half-hour waiting for someone to put in an appearance.'

'Dad's still at work, Mom's round at her sister's and I've been for a walk,' she explained, still in shock. 'If you'll give me a minute to return Max to his owners. It's only next door.'

'Carry on,' he invited. 'I'll wait.'

Kerry turned the animal over, exchanged a few words with her neighbour—who had known her since she was a baby—and made her way back to where she had left Lee. He straightened away from the car door where he had been leaning, stamping his feet to restore circulation obviously impeded by his lack of suitable footwear.

'I've known it colder, but not much,' he remarked.
'Beautiful countryside though.'

'Your first time up here?' Kerry asked, leading the
way up the garden path.

'First time in the Dales.'

They were making polite conversation like two strangers, she thought, sliding her key into the door lock. She
was vitally aware of him at her back—and churned up
inside over his being here at all. What could he possibly
have to say to her that couldn't be said over the phone?

The warmth of central heating welcomed them indoors. Kerry slipped off her anorak and boots, then held
out a hand for the sheepskin Lee had already shed.

'The sitting room's through there.' She indicated the
nearest door. 'Make yourself at home while I hang these
up. I'll make some tea—unless you'd prefer coffee?'

Lee shook his head. 'Tea sounds fine.'

He made no attempt to follow her directions but
waited until she had hung both coats away in the under-
stairs closet and donned a pair of low-heeled pumps,
then accompanied her through to the kitchen at the rear
of the house.

Dressed casually in fawn cord trousers and white roll-
necked sweater, he looked totally at ease as he leaned a
hip against a work-surface to watch her fill the kettle
and plug it in.

Acutely conscious of her lack of make-up, tousled hair
and shabby old jeans and sweater, Kerry felt anything
but at ease. He had seen her looking less than her best
before, of course, but the circumstances had been somewhat different. What he must be thinking now, she didn't
care to imagine.

'We usually have supper around six-thirty,' she said,
'but I can make you a sandwich if you're hungry.'

'Assuming I'm invited to supper, I can hold out for a
couple of hours,' he returned. 'But first and foremost...'

Kerry went rigid as he took hold of her, but not for long. His mouth compelled an answer. Her mind whirling, she gave it, feeling the warmth of his arms around her—the hard strength of his body.

'Worth the journey on its own!' he declared moments later.

'I can still hardly believe you made it,' she murmured, still struggling to contain the emotions he had aroused in her.

'You need further proof?' There was amusement in his voice.

Kerry forced a laugh. 'Just a figure of speech. You feel real enough.'

'I should hope so.' Lee held her far enough away from him to study her, his eyes penetrating her guard. 'What was all that about not accepting my Christmas present?'

She hesitated, not sure how exactly to put it. 'If it had been something simple I might have.'

His brows drew together. 'You mean in worth?'

'Well…yes.'

'Most women would be insulted by a cheap present.'

'I'm not most women.'

'So I keep discovering.' The following pause was lengthy, his unwavering gaze bringing colour to her cheeks. 'You really want me to take the watch back?'

'If they'll do it.'

'I dare say.' He didn't sound concerned with that aspect. His hands came up to cup her face in a manner only too reminiscent of another time and place, his expression difficult to define. 'I've missed you, Kerry. More than I anticipated.'

The kettle's boiling,' she said thickly. 'It doesn't have automatic cut-out.'

'It isn't on its own,' came the answer, but he released her. 'Make the tea if you must.'

She did so, controlling the shakiness in her limbs with

difficulty. There had to be more to his coming all this way than her refusal to accept the watch, but what exactly? Leopards didn't change their spots; he almost certainly hadn't altered his basic philosophy.

What was more likely was a reluctance to let a woman be the one to do the dumping—hence the attempt to seduce her with expensive gifts. Male pride was what it all boiled down to, nothing more. Well, no matter how much effort he put into it, she wasn't falling for it, she told herself forcefully.

He carried the tray through to the sitting room, reminding her of the first time he had visited the flat. It seemed a long time ago, but it wasn't. Little more than two weeks, in fact. It hardly seemed possible.

With the curtains drawn against the night and the fire she had left banked up casting flickering shadows, the room took on a cosy intimacy. The tea had been a gesture, Kerry was bound to admit. She didn't want it, and was pretty sure Lee didn't either. Seated in the roomy armchair opposite—his features bronzed by the firelight—he made her ache with a longing she fought to subdue.

'Does Estelle know where you are?' she asked, desperate for something—anything—to say.

He shook his head. 'She thinks I'm in Bristol overnight. It's where I'm supposed to be, as a matter of fact, but I just kept driving.'

'How did you know where to come?'

'I contacted Jane before she left on Christmas Eve. She gave me the number and address.'

Green eyes focussed more intently. 'You mean you'd already decided then on making this trip?'

'Only the phone call Christmas morning at that point. It was Jane's idea to give me the address. As I said, I set off this morning with Bristol in mind. Consciously, at any rate.'

'Business meeting?'

'No, visiting friends. I phoned to tell them I couldn't make it when I stopped for lunch.'

The intimation that she had proved the greater draw was warming, despite her doubts as to its sincerity. Kerry forced herself to take an objective view. Lee was no creature of impulse—everything he did had a design. Right now he was out to get her. Once he had her where he wanted her he would choose his own time to end things—the way he always had. Apart from Renata, that was.

'Did you phone here from Winster?' she asked.

If Lee registered any undertones in the question he gave no sign of it. 'Yes, I did. We spent three days there.'

'I imagine Renata makes a big thing of it all.'

'Rather more than Philip would, left to his own devices. The staff were going down like ninepins with flu when we left so the New Year's Eve party has had to be called off.'

'That's a pity. It must have taken a lot of planning.'

'No doubt.' He paused, then added softly, 'Why don't you come over here? We probably don't have much time before your parents arrive home.'

'About twenty minutes before Dad gets in,' she confirmed, repressing the sudden reckless inclination to do as he said regardless. 'Mom could be back any time.'

'I wasn't suggesting an orgy,' he returned drily. 'I happen to enjoy kissing you.'

As a prelude, Kerry reflected with cynicism. Tension sharpened her voice.

'You didn't come all this way for a few kisses, Lee.'

Something flickered in the grey eyes but his voice, when he answered, was level enough. 'That's true. I'm here to sort things out between us.'

'To what purpose?' she challenged, taking the bull by the horns.

'A view to the future,' he returned steadily. 'The long-term future, I hope.'

Were there no depths to which he wouldn't stoop? Kerry wondered contemptuously, refusing to allow herself even a momentary hesitation. Did he really think her gullible enough to fall for such a line?

'Oh, of course!' she said, sarcasm dripping from her tongue. 'What else could you possibly have in mind? You'll be asking me to marry you next!'

His smile was faint. 'As I said before, stranger things have happened.'

'Such as pigs taking to the air!' Her head thrown back and with eyes sparkling like twin emeralds, Kerry curled a derisive lip. 'Have another try!'

For a long moment he sat there, studying her with an expression that made her quail suddenly inside. When he moved it was with deliberation, getting up from the chair to cross to where she sat and yank her to her feet. His hands were hard, bringing her up to him, his mouth a searing demand that brooked no resistance.

In spite of everything, she found herself responding, helpless to turn off the heat spiralling upwards and outwards to every extremity. She was aware with every fibre of the growing pressure of his arousal—wanting him with a hunger that nullified all other concerns. She moved her body instinctively against him, moaning deep in her throat at the exquisite sensation.

'*Now* tell me you don't want me!' he said roughly, grinding her even closer.

Mindful suddenly of where they were, she made a valiant effort to recover some control, her voice low and shaky. 'Let me go, Lee. Please!'

'I'll let you go,' he said, 'when *I've* a mind to do it.' He ran one hand up her back to tangle it in the length

of chestnut hair, making her gasp as he pulled her head
none too gently back until she was gazing directly into
his face. There was anger in his eyes, a hard tension in
the line of his jaw.

'I didn't follow you up here to get kicked in the gut.
I came because I believed we might have something
worth going out on a limb for.'

Another line, she told herself, but there was no conviction in it. She gazed at him like a child at a problem
picture, wanting to believe what he appeared to be saying but afraid to let her defences down any further than
they had already fallen.

'Such as what?' she got out.

He drew in an impatient breath. 'Don't play games.
You know as well as I do what.'

'All I know,' she said, 'is that you obviously still have
the hots for me!'

The fingers still entangled in her hair tightened their
grip painfully, the glitter in the grey eyes a warning of
worse to come if she goaded him any further. 'If all I
was after was sex I could have found it a lot nearer home
than this!'

The sound of a key in the front door lock stilled any
reply. Not that she was sure what she would have said
to that last in any case, Kerry conceded as Lee released
her abruptly.

'We'll finish this later,' he stated with emphasis.

Obviously prepared for a visitor by the car parked at
the gate, Ann Pierson took in the firelit scene with curiosity obvious in her expression. Kerry made haste to
perform introductions.

'Mom, I'd like you to meet Lee Hartford.'

'We already spoke on the phone Christmas Day,' said
the latter, his tone easy again. 'Hello again, Mrs
Pierson.'

Looking thoroughly bemused, Ann shook the hand extended to her. 'This is a surprise,' she said, then added, glancing across at her daughter, 'Or is it?'

Lee answered for her. 'Kerry didn't know I was coming. A last-minute decision on my part.'

'A long way to come on the spur of the moment.' It was more of a statement than a question. 'Nice to meet you, anyway, Mr Hartford.'

'Lee,' he said. 'I can see where Kerry gets her looks.'

Ann smiled and shook her head. 'My sister's the one she takes after most.' She looked back at her daughter. 'Did you do anything about supper?'

'The hotpot's in the oven, and I made an apricot pie this morning which only needs reheating,' Kerry confirmed. 'Enough for four,' she tagged on, with the barest of glances in Lee's direction. 'Unless you'd prefer not to, of course.'

'I'd be delighted,' he said. 'The hotpot sounds intriguing.'

'It's just a stew with potatoes cooked in with it,' she explained, not about to start apologising for the simplicity of the fare. 'Filling and warming on a cold winter's night. I'll go and change before Dad gets home.'

Upstairs in her bedroom she took off the jeans and donned a swirling blue skirt, exchanging the thick Shetland sweater for a lighter weight in cream. Bare of make-up, the face in the mirror had patches of colour high on the cheek-bones and there was a glitter in the green eyes.

A cynic, Lee had called her, but didn't she have every excuse for being one where he was concerned? He'd led Sarah to believe he had long-term interest in her, and look where *she* was. Whatever his motives in chasing after her this way, they most certainly didn't include marriage plans. Not that she had any desire to marry him, anyway. No woman with any sense at all would put her trust in a man like him.

If his appearance had been a shock for her it must have been doubly so for her mother, she realised, coming home to find the man her daughter had denied having any serious involvement with right here in the house.

Her father's reactions she wasn't at all sure about. He knew about both phone call and present because her mother had told the whole family over lunch the same day, but all he'd said was that it was her own affair not theirs.

He hadn't exactly washed his hands of her when she had moved to London, just told her that if she did go whatever happened to her was on her own head.

How true, she thought now. If she hadn't fancied her chances in the retaliation department to start with she wouldn't be in this position.

Her father came in as she was descending the stairs. Stockily built and balding, his face dour in repose, he both looked and acted older than his fifty-five years. Kerry couldn't remember him ever being any different, although her mother always claimed he'd been a bit of a rogue in his youth.

'Who's the car belong to?' he asked without preamble.

'Lee Hartford drove up to see me,' Kerry told him, seeing no point in beating about the bush either. 'Come and meet him.'

Never stuck for a word or two, her mother was chatting away comfortably when they went through to the sitting room. Lee rose from his chair to offer a hand to the older man, who shook it somewhat perfunctorily.

'Business slack?' he asked gruffly.

'There's never much doing between Christmas and New Year,' Lee agreed.

'Not much doing any time of year up here. Whole country's going to the dogs, if you ask me!'

'I'll go and lay the table,' Kerry mouthed to her

mother, unwilling to stand by listening to her father expound on his pet subject.

Setting out place mats in the small but nicely furnished dining room, she could hear her father's voice droning on and felt fleeting sympathy for Lee who was having to bear the brunt of it. Not that he appeared to be taking it all quietly—she could hear his voice, too, from time to time, although not the actual words.

Ann came through to join her, grinning from ear to ear. 'Dad's met his match in that man of yours!' she announced.

'He isn't *my* man,' Kerry responded, and saw her mother's expression turn bland.

'Of course not. Do you know how long he's planning on staying?'

'I hadn't even thought about it.'

'Well, I don't imagine he's going to be driving all that way back tonight, at any rate. I can always make up the spare room.'

'If he stays at all I'd think he'd prefer a hotel,' Kerry said hastily.

Ann smiled comfortably. 'Well, we'll see, shall we? I'll get the hotpot while you call them through.'

Whatever the differences in opinion might be, things seemed amicable enough on the surface when the men put in an appearance. Lee sniffed appreciatively at the savoury aroma coming from the casserole dish, placed ready for serving directly onto the plates.

'I didn't realise how hungry I was until now,' he admitted. 'That smells wonderful!'

'Kerry was always a good cook,' said Ann. 'Just wait till you taste her pastry!'

Grey eyes met green, dark brows tilting. 'A woman of many talents, your daughter. My mother would be lost without her.'

'Any competent stenographer could take dictation,' Kerry responded levelly.

'But not necessarily with the same amount of interest and encouragement. She'd have given up that first week if you hadn't persuaded her to carry on.'

'It was too good a job to let go so soon.'

'Whatever you say.'

Watching the two of them, Frank Pierson seemed on the verge of saying something himself, but apparently thought better of it. For a man who didn't normally care much for company outside his own family circle he was showing surprisingly little resentment of the intrusion, Kerry reflected.

Lee devoured two helpings of the stew, and another two of the pie. He hadn't, he declared afterwards, enjoyed anything as much in a long time.

'You'll have to show Mrs Ralston how to make a Yorkshire hotpot,' he said.

'It's a Lancashire dish, actually,' Kerry advised, unable to imagine herself instructing the housekeeper in any such thing. 'We can't even call Yorkshire pudding our own invention. That recipe originated in France.'

'Only according to some,' defended her mother.

Hardly a scintillating topic, Kerry thought wryly. Any more than her father's discourse on greyhound racing had been during the meal. Lee must be bored out of his mind by now. Not that he showed it, of course. She stole a glance at him, to see an enigmatic little smile on his lips. If only she could read what was really going on in that dark head!

Her father's suggestion that the two of them pop down to the local pub while the women cleared away induced a quizzical lift of an eyebrow in her direction, though his agreement came readily enough.

'You'll not be thinking of driving back tonight, will

you?' queried Ann. 'We've a spare room only needs making up.'

'That's very good of you,' he acknowledged without hesitation. 'Bears out everything I've heard about Yorkshire hospitality.'

'You're more than welcome,' she said, looking gratified. 'If you've nothing with you I can find you a pair of Frank's pyjamas.'

Kerry was hard put to it to control a sudden gurgle of laughter at the mental image of that lean muscularity clad in traditional striped cotton made for a man several inches shorter and quite a lot wider in hip and waist. She doubted if Lee wore pyjamas at all, if it came to that.

'I've an overnight case in the car, thanks,' he said easily. 'I was intending to book into a hotel. I'll fetch it in when we get back.'

Kerry began gathering plates as the two men went to get their coats. If her father followed his usual Thursday night routine he would be playing darts, which meant they wouldn't be back before closing time. Hardly the kind of evening entertainment Lee was used to, but no doubt he would cope. In the meantime, she had to get her head straight.

Carrying the plates through to the kitchen, she ran hot water into the bowl and added washing-up liquid. Her mother followed her in with the serving dishes, eyeing her questioningly.

'You're not upset because your father asked him to go to the pub, are you?' she asked.

'More surprised,' Kerry admitted. 'Dad isn't usually so forthcoming with strangers.'

'I know. I was surprised, too. Especially feeling the way he generally does about southerners. You'd think it was two different countries!'

In some ways, Kerry could have told her, it was. Certainly the life she lived down there bore little resemblance to what she had known up here. It might have been better if she'd never left. Safer in many respects, for sure.

It was close to eleven when the two men finally returned. Kerry had rarely seen her father looking so cheerful.

'Plays a mean game of darts, this chap,' he exclaimed. 'A real mean game! We wiped the floor with the Pig and Whistle!'

'Sheer luck on my part,' disclaimed Lee.

'Anyway, I'm off to bed,' declared the older man. 'Your mother already gone, has she?'

'About ten minutes ago,' Kerry confirmed.

'Right, I'll say goodnight, then.'

Silence reigned for a moment or two after the door closed in his wake. Kerry was the first to break it, unable to sustain the tension. 'You seem to have made quite an impression.'

Lee shrugged. 'He isn't such a hard man to get along with. We had quite a chat between times.'

'About what?' she asked.

'You and me,' he said. 'He wanted to know what my intentions were.'

'I'm sure you told him.'

Hands in pockets and stance relaxed, he inclined his head. 'I told him we were giving ourselves time. He seemed to understand that—even appreciate it. No point in rushing things, he said. Get to know one another first the way he and your mother did.'

'Go to hell!' She gave the invective everything she had, recognising mockery when she heard it. 'Just go to hell, Lee!'

'Not right now, thanks,' he returned equably. 'Did anyone ever tell you you're quite magnificent when you're angry? Irresistible, in fact.'

Kerry forced herself to stand still as he shifted with

obvious purpose, but she couldn't stop the rush of blood to her head when he took hold of her.

'Stop it!' she jerked out through lips gone stiff with tension. 'Leave me alone!'

'You don't want that any more than I do,' he said, 'so stop protesting. I told you we'd finish this later.'

He hooked her legs from under her, lowering her to the thick-piled hearthrug in the same smooth movement and coming down with her, his face devilish in the flickering firelight. He caught her wrists and held them in one hand as she made to rake her nails down his face. Kerry gazed up at him helplessly, unable to deny the pulsing thrill as he used his other hand to trace a slow path down the length of her body.

'Say it,' he commanded.

'Say what?' she choked, hardly able to stand the sensations created by those long, lean, knowing fingers.

'I want you, Lee. More than I ever wanted anyone. *Say* it!' he insisted.

His hand slid up under her skirt, caressing the soft inner flesh of her thigh. She drew in a shuddering breath as he brushed the back of a finger across the taut strip of lace-edged cotton which was her only protection, feeling the sudden contraction—the aching need.

'I want you, Lee,' she whispered, past putting up any further resistance.

'More than that,' he insisted, subtly increasing the pressure. 'A whole lot more.'

'I *want* you!' Her jaw was clenched, her every nerve ending directly connected to that central point. 'You know I do, damn you! I want you,' she repeated on a softer, almost pleading note.

'Unfortunately, you're not going to get me,' he said on a note of regret. 'Not now, at any rate. It would be abusing your mother's hospitality.'

'*Louse!*' In that moment, Kerry knew what it felt like to want to commit murder. 'You set me up!'

He held her easily as she attempted to push herself upright, shaking his head in mock reproof. 'Not so much noise! Do you want your parents coming down to see what's going on?'

The very idea was enough to quieten her. She lay glaring helplessly up at him.

'That's better,' he said. 'Much better.'

He dropped his head to seek her lips with his, defeating her attempt to twist her head away from him. There was no closing him out—and after a moment no desire left to even try. Her arms rose without conscious volition to slide about his neck, her fingers curving into the thick dark hair. She wasn't thinking now, only feeling—and the feeling was overpowering.

Once again it was Lee who called a halt. 'Much as I'd like to carry on, I think we'd better cool off,' he said softly. 'Your parents deserve better.'

Whereas she deserved exactly what she got, thought Kerry wryly, cursing her weakness. Lee had her right where he had intended, helpless to resist him.

'Let me up,' she said, voice low. 'You proved your point.'

'Being what?' he asked, making no move.

'That I'm a walk-over when it comes right down to it—like all the rest.'

The muscles around his mouth tautened suddenly, his teeth coming together with an audible snap. 'I haven't driven over two hundred miles just to prove a point, for God's sake! I already told you why I'm here. What do I have to do to convince you?'

Kerry gazed at him irresolutely, torn by conflicting emotions. A part of her wanted badly to believe what he appeared to be saying, while the other, saner part re-

minded her of Sarah's downfall. She could all too easily
finish up the same way.

'I'm not sure,' she admitted. 'I'm not sure of anything
right now.' She put a tentative hand up to his lips, tracing the firm lines with an unsteady fingertip. 'I'm still
getting over the shock of you turning up here at all.'

The anger was still there, but lacking its initial force.
'You could say I was under an inexorable compulsion.'
He studied her vibrant face, his expression relaxing a
little. 'How about coming back with me tomorrow?'

'Why?' she got out.

'Because I want to see the New Year in with you.'

'What about your mother?'

'She's spending the night with friends.'

And where, Kerry wondered, did he intend *they*
should spend the night? The answer, of course, was obvious. With his mother out of the way, what better opportunity?

'Well?' he urged.

'You're hardly short of friends yourself,' she said. 'I
doubt if you'll be lonely.'

Lee drew in a short, hard breath. 'Cut it out, will you?
I asked a straight question. I want a straight answer. Are
you coming back with me?'

Kerry gave in, unable to form an outright refusal when
the greater part of her wanted so much to say yes. 'I
suppose so.'

'Such enthusiasm,' he mocked, but there was no bite
to it. He got lithely to his feet, reaching down a hand to
haul her to hers—holding her there for a moment to
probe the darkened green eyes. 'No changing your mind.
I won't stand for it. And, in case you're wondering how
your parents are going to feel about you leaving early,
I already told your father. He didn't raise any objections.'

'Supposing I'd said no?' she queried.

'I wasn't going to take no for an answer.' He smiled at the expression on her face. 'We'll be making an early start so we'd both better get some sleep. Just point me to the right room.'

She did so, half disappointed, half relieved when he made no attempt to touch her again. However genuine he appeared to be about all this, she still found it difficult to put Sarah's experience from mind. What she mustn't do was allow her feelings for him to get out of hand the way Sarah had done. Enjoy what there was and walk away from it when the time came. That was the best philosophy.

CHAPTER NINE

THE snow petered out after they left the Dales region, though grey skies and driving rain hardly made for a pleasant journey. It was gone five when they finally reached London.

With Jane still on Christmas leave herself and the flat unheated for a week, it had never seemed more unwelcoming. Kerry knew little hesitation when Lee suggested that she gather what she needed and go straight on home with him. Having come this far, she may as well go the whole hog, she thought drily. At the very least it would be warm.

Mrs Ralston greeted the pair of them without surprise. Hardly the first time Lee had brought someone home with him, Kerry suspected, despite his implicit denial when she had brought the subject up on the way to the Lattimers' party. Sarah had never actually mentioned visiting the house at any time but that wasn't to say she hadn't been here.

She put the thought aside swiftly. The last person she needed reminding of right now was Sarah.

Shown to the same room she had used the last time, she unpacked the few things she had brought with her, then took a leisurely shower—luxuriating in the endless supply of hot water. There was every possibility that she would be sharing the next shower with Lee, a thought which brought an anticipatory quiver.

She visualised his fine, naked body glistening with water, his taunting grey eyes and sensual mouth—his whole dynamic personality. Trying to persuade herself that she could walk away unscathed if he did turn out

142

to be simply playing the power game with her was a waste of time, she admitted ruefully. For better or worse, she was in love with the man.

The bronze silk dress she had brought with her wasn't new but still had plenty of life left in it. Long, it fell in a soft flare from a fitted waist, the deep V-neckline revealing a modest amount of cleavage. Lee eyed her approvingly when she went down to join him for a drink in the drawing room, before setting out for the evening.

'You look lovely,' he said. He brought across the gin and tonic she had requested, tilting her chin with a fingertip to press a tantalisingly fleeting kiss on her lips before handing over the glass. 'Then, you never look anything but.'

Hardly first thing in the morning with mascara all over her face, Kerry reflected in semi-humorous recollection. Tonight she would make sure to remove it before going to sleep.

Given the opportunity, came the mental rider, sending a tremor down her spine.

'Where are we supposed to be going?' she asked, putting all such thoughts firmly aside for the present.

'The usual duty call first,' he said, taking a seat on the sofa beside her.

The staff party, Kerry remembered with suddenly sinking heart. He always paid a visit to the staff party on New Year's Eve.

Lee was looking at her oddly. 'Something wrong?'

'I did holiday cover at your place last year,' she admitted. 'I'll probably know several people who'll be there tonight.'

'Fine. You can renew acquaintances.' He reached out a hand to wind a tendril of bright hair round a finger, his eyes roving her face. 'How come I missed seeing you? I'd certainly have remembered.'

'I was just one of many.' She squashed the thought

that the same might still be said of now, too, her every sense alive to his touch. 'I never saw you either, if it comes to that. Temporary staff don't normally have reason to come up to the executive floor.'

'I suppose not.'

Taking the glass from her unresisting hand, he deposited it along with his own on the nearby table, then drew her closer to put his lips to her temple. Kerry closed her eyes as he feathered kisses slowly down the line of her cheek to reach her mouth, feeling the heady tension spreading through her body.

'We've a lot of lost time to make up for,' he murmured. 'Maybe we should stay and see the New Year in right here.'

'The staff will be expecting you,' she reminded him unsteadily.

'I shouldn't imagine it will make much difference to them whether I show up or not,' he said, 'but maybe you're right. Anything worth having is worth waiting for.' He let her go, reaching for the glass he had so recently set down. 'Drink up, and we'll get off. I booked a table for dinner.'

If he was put out by the rebuff he was concealing it pretty well. It was too early for love-making, anyway, Kerry told herself, and wondered who she was trying to kid. What she'd really wanted was for Lee to override her. So much for feminism! she thought ironically.

Walking in on the revelry of the staff party some little time later, it was inevitable that the first person she laid eyes on should turn out to be Jason King. The latter's expression spoke volumes for his thoughts, an opinion which was, no doubt, shared by others. In all fairness, Kerry couldn't really blame them. The way they saw it she was just the latest in a long line of Hartford acquisitions.

Cornering her while Lee was engaged in conversation

with a couple of the senior staff, Jason got his dig in
right away.

'He had a blonde with him last year. I wonder what
colour will be in favour next year!'

'I can't foretell the future, I'm afraid,' Kerry responded equably, determined not to let him get to her.

'*I* can,' he sneered. 'I'd give you a month at the long-
est.'

'*You* couldn't give me anything,' she returned with an
edge she couldn't quite eradicate.

A flush suffused the good-looking features. 'I don't
have the same kind of money, that's for sure! Better get
what you can out of him while it lasts. He's supposed
to be pretty generous with his women.'

Kerry bit her lip as he sauntered away, aware of letting herself down by rising to the bait even as far as she
had. Not that he'd told her anything she didn't already
know. She hadn't yet found the right moment to return
the watch Lee had bought her, though she still had no
intention of keeping it. Money was the last thing she
wanted from him.

As he had already indicated, his appearance was little
more than a token gesture. She was only too ready to
comply when he suggested they left.

'You didn't seem too comfortable in there,' he observed in the taxi he'd kept waiting for the past half-
hour.

'I felt a bit awkward,' Kerry admitted. 'From holiday
cover to this... Well, you have to see it from their side.'

'No, I don't. It isn't their business.' He gave her a
shrewd glance. 'Did you and King have something going
when you were there?'

Did he know *all* the staff by name? Kerry wondered
fleetingly. 'I went out with him once,' she admitted. 'We
didn't...see eye to eye.'

Lee slanted a lip. 'You mean you sent him for an early

bath, too? I don't imagine that happens to him too often.
He has a reputation as the office Lothario.'

It takes one to know one, flashed across Kerry's mind.
The intimation that she had been giving him the same
kind of treatment earlier stung too much to let it pass.
'He took rather too much for granted,' she said coolly.
'A major fault with some men.'

His profile hard-edged against the street lighting, Lee
gave a short laugh. 'Message received.'

'I wasn't referring to you,' she denied on a subdued
note, wishing she'd kept her mouth shut.

'Yes, you were. You're probably right, too. I had but
the one thought in mind at the time, I admit. The difference between male and female priorities.'

Meaning she was more interested in going out on the
town, Kerry surmised. She opened her mouth to deny it,
then closed it again, realising the futility. The only way
she was going to convince him was to tell him what
she'd really wanted, and there was no way she was doing
that!

Any constraint between them faded over dinner. The
food was superb, the wine like nectar, the whole ambience stimulating. By the end of the meal Kerry was on
a high she had no intention of coming down from.

Lit by the soft glow of the table-lamp set between
them, Lee's face seemed carved from bronze—his
breadth of shoulder shutting out the room beyond. On
impulse, she reached across to take the lean-fingered
hand resting on the white cloth and turn it over, contemplating the lines spread across his palm.

'You have a very strong lifeline,' she declared, tracing
it with the tip of a delicate pink nail. 'A long one, too.'

'You read palms often?' he asked.

'Only when I feel the vibes strongly enough,' she
quipped. 'You give off a powerful aura.'

'Maybe time I changed my aftershave.' He made no

attempt to withdraw his hand. 'So, what else do you see?'

'Success, of course,' she said. 'Increasing all the way through!'

'How about my private life?'

Looking up to meet his enigmatic gaze, Kerry took care to keep her tone light. 'There's a limit to what an amateur palmist can glean, I'm afraid.'

'Too bad. It was just getting interesting.' He closed his fingers on hers and rubbed the ball of his thumb softly over the backs, his mouth curving. 'Maybe the vibes need a boost.'

They couldn't be coming across any more forcefully than they were right now, she thought, every nerve ending in her prickling to his touch. Not that it made him any easier to plumb. *Did* he really care about her, or was she simply another Sarah?

'You could always try sticking a finger in the bulb socket,' she suggested with a smile she hoped didn't look as forced to him as it felt to her.

He laughed. 'I can think of better ways of getting lit up!'

Kerry could imagine. He would be putting them into practice before long, too. Forget the future and concentrate on the present, she told herself resolutely. If this turned out to be all there was then this was what she would have to settle for.

It was gone ten-thirty when they left the restaurant. Contrary to her expectations, Lee didn't suggest going straight back to the house but instructed the taxi driver to take them on to Churchills.

The nightclub was packed but they were obviously expected, seats having been kept for them at a long table already occupied by people Kerry recognised from the Lattimers' party. Seeing Renata herself there was deflating, although she did her best to put a good face on it. With the fancy-dress party cancelled, it was hardly to be expected that the Lattimers would stay home for the evening.

Renata certainly didn't appear to be entertaining any regrets about the cancellation. Stunning in red, she offered Kerry the briefest of greetings then totally ignored her and concentrated her attention on Lee.

Watching the two of them when they eventually danced together, Kerry was even more certain that her suspicions regarding their previous relationship were well founded. There was intimacy in the very way they came together—her arms about his neck, face lifted to his, mouth a luscious red temptation.

Impossible as it was to tell what Lee was thinking or feeling, he was certainly making no attempt to ease her away from him. It would, Kerry judged, be difficult to slide a sheet of A4 between the pair of them!

She was reluctant to accept when Philip asked her to dance but could find no adequate reason to refuse. The floor was thronged, movement of any kind difficult. Philip held her close because there was no room to do otherwise, though with a great deal more circumspection than his wife and friend were demonstrating.

'I'm really glad you decided to come back for New Year,' he said. I've never known Lee as restless as he was over Christmas. He missed you badly.'

Kerry felt her heart jerk. 'He told you that?'

'He didn't need to tell me. I've known him a long time.'

Her laugh was brittle. 'He doesn't seem to be missing me much at the moment!'

Immediately she'd said it she regretted it, although Philip could hardly be unaware of what she was talking about. 'Ignore that,' she tagged on hastily. 'I'm reading too much into too little.'

'Not on my wife's part.' Philip sounded matter-of-fact about it. 'With her it's always been Lee.'

Kerry looked up at him in bewilderment. 'Then why—?'

'She wanted the title, *I* wanted her. Still do,' he added with a hint of irony.

'It doesn't bother you that she...feels the way she does about Lee?'

'It might if I thought there was anything going on between them.'

'You mean you trust them both?'

'I trust Lee.'

Kerry cast a glance to where the other couple could just be glimpsed through the moving throng. They were, she noted grimly, no further apart.

'Don't take it to heart,' Philip advised, accurately gauging her expression. 'It's quite difficult to disentangle a woman who's intent on staying close.'

'Especially when the contact isn't exactly unwelcome to start with!'

'A fact of life, I'm afraid. It's a rare man who doesn't enjoy tactile contact with a beautiful woman. I'm no exception myself.'

Looking up to catch the teasing twinkle in his eyes, Kerry gave a reluctant smile. 'You certainly know how to flatter!'

'No flattery,' he assured her. 'You're lovely to look at *and* to hold. Intelligent, too. Lee would be a fool to let you get away from him.'

The music came to a stop before she could come up with an answer to that—if there was an answer. She accompanied Philip back to the table to see Lee settling Renata back into her seat with a murmur in her ear that brought a smile to the red lips, and she wished she could share the other man's faith.

Given the opportunity to make love to a woman as

beautiful as Renata—and there seemed little doubt that
she would willingly provide the opportunity—then it
was surely a rare man who would refuse to indulge himself.

As to Philip himself, how he could have married the
woman at all, knowing that she didn't love him, was
beyond all reckoning. Was the physical side all *any* of
them really cared about?

With the memory of Renata's curves pressed so close
to Lee still sharp in her mind, she found it impossible
to relax when Lee took her onto the floor some time
later. Feeling her rigidity, he looked down at her with
quizzically lifted brows.

'Something I said?'

'It's too hot in here for smooching,' she declared
shortly.

'Smooching!' He sounded more amused than annoyed. 'Now there's a word I haven't heard used in a
long time!'

'So I'm outdated,' she clipped back, losing what little
cool she had left. 'Better than acting like a bitch on
heat!'

Regretting the words if not the sentiment, she was
thrown to feel him shake with sudden laughter.

'Don't hold back,' he said. 'Tell it the way it is!' He
tightened his hold on her as she made an instinctive
movement away from him, looking down into her taut
face with the merriment still glinting in his eyes. 'No
flouncing off in high dudgeon, as they say. That would
embarrass us both.'

'I doubt if anything could embarrass *you*!' she
snapped.

'It's been known.' He ran a hand slowly up her spine,
smiling at her involuntary shudder. 'Good to know you
care enough to get angry over my paying attention to
another woman.'

The raillery cut deep, lending extra bite to her voice. 'You can pay attention to as many other women as you like. I'm angry for Philip. He's supposed to be your friend!'

'He is. The closest I've got.'

'Then leave his wife alone!'

'There's nothing going on between Renata and me, if that's what you're implying,' he denied, sounding a great deal less humorous himself now.

'That isn't how it looks.'

'It's what I'm telling you.'

'And your word is your bond, of course!' Kerry was past caring what she said, intent only on piercing that hide of his. 'I doubt if Sarah Hartley would put her trust in it again!'

There was no immediate answer but she felt the change in him—the sudden hardness of the hands at her back. When he did speak it was with a quietness more ominous than any anger.

'A friend of yours, I take it?'

It was too late to retract, even if she'd wanted to, Kerry acknowledged fatalistically. Why not get it all out while she was about it, anyway?

'We shared a flat when I first came to London,' she said. 'Our lifestyles don't overlap all that often these days.'

'But you obviously know we were involved some time back.'

'Obviously.'

'And would that have had anything to do with your attitude towards me when we first met?'

Kerry steeled herself against the momentary hesitation. Whatever regrets she might have afterwards, she had gone too far to back down now.

'It had some bearing,' she confirmed. 'What you did to Sarah—'

'Whatever she told you, it was evidently enough to set your back up pretty thoroughly,' Lee interrupted flatly. 'Which rather begs the question of why you changed your mind about me.' The pause was timed. 'Or did you?'

The arms holding her were like bands of steel across her back. Kerry swallowed on the dryness in her throat, wishing she had never started this.

'What was the plan?' he continued inexorably when she failed to answer. 'To give me the run-around on Sarah's behalf?'

'Something like that,' she admitted with reluctance.

There was a hint of cruelty in the curl of his lip. 'It didn't get very far, did it?'

The allusion was obvious, her response instinctive. 'It got *this* far!'

His jaw tautened as the implication went home, his eyes turning to cold hard steel. When he spoke his voice was equally cold. 'Timing is all-important when delivering the *coup de grâce*. Didn't anyone ever tell you that? You're a little too early for full impact.'

The anger and resentment had vanished, replaced by a numb wretchedness. 'Lee...' she began, her voice fading away in recognition of the unlikelihood of his listening to any denials now. She had talked herself into a corner there was no getting out of.

She was sick of the whole charade anyway, she told herself hollowly. Lee had no feeling for her; all he'd really wanted was a bedmate for the night. He could have found one elsewhere, of course, but that wouldn't have been half as satisfying to his ego as fetching her to heel—as he'd thought. She was well out of it.

As if in mockery, the music stopped and the ten-second countdown to midnight began, culminating in a frenzy of cheers as the old year ended and the new one

arrived. Kerry stiffened involuntarily as Lee drew her up
to him, seeing the ruthless look in his eyes.

'Happy New Year, darling!' he said with irony.

The kiss was long and demanding, the hands at her
back moulding her to every hard angle of his body.
Kerry knew an almost uncontrollable urge to bite his lip,
refraining only because she suspected he might very well
bite her back. Early or not, she had made a dent in his
pride that had to be avenged. At least he knew now what
it was like to be on the receiving end.

Philip in tow, Renata was there beside them when he
let her go as abruptly as he had seized her.

'Share and share alike!' declared the other woman
with a glance that challenged Kerry to dissent.

Philip's kiss was light, his smile rallying. 'Happy New
Year, Kerry.'

Behind him, his wife was putting heart and soul into
an embrace which left no doubt at all of her inclinations.
On the face of it Lee seemed to be doing rather more
taking than giving, but probably only because Philip was
in the vicinity. Kerry dredged up a smile of her own,
determined not to give way to the pain deep in her chest.

'Happy New Year!' she echoed.

The noise around them was deafening, the revellers
obviously only just getting into their stride. The thought
of another hour or two of this was suffocating. Not that
she had to stick it out, of course. Lee might not appreciate her walking out on him in front of everyone but
he could hardly force her to stay if she decided otherwise.

In any case, she certainly wouldn't be going back to
the house with him now. She'd take a taxi straight back
to the flat.

Having settled her mind to it, it came as something
of a shock when he intimated that he was ready to go
himself. Renata looked dropped-on, too.

Viewing Lee's unmoved expression as the woman remonstrated with him, Kerry thought that while they might well have been lovers before she married Philip it was doubtful if what Louise Strickland had told her about his wanting to marry the lovely blonde himself really held water. No one woman would ever matter that much to him.

Whether ordered in advance or simply a fortuitous appearance, there was a taxi waiting when they got outside. The skies were clear, the streets crowded with merrymakers, the whole atmosphere one of temporary goodwill. Looking from the cab window, Kerry wished she was out there with them—wished she was anywhere right now but here with the man seated silently at her side.

'Would it be easier to drop you off first or go straight to Battersea?' she asked tonelessly.

'Wherever we go we go together,' Lee stated, drawing her head sharply round.

'There's no reason for me to come back with you now.'

A mirthless smile crossed the lean features. 'I'd say we owed it to each other to finish the night out.'

Kerry gazed at him in disbelief, thankful that the glass partition between driver and passenger compartments was fully closed. 'You must be mad if you think I'm going to spend the night with you!'

'Try me,' he invited. 'We made the arrangement, we stick to it.'

'Not on your life!' she snarled at him. 'You've already had all you're going to get out of me!'

'A matter of opinion.' His eyes cold in the light from the streetlamps, his mouth sardonic, he looked immovable. 'You play the game, you pay the price.'

She said thickly, 'It wasn't a game.'

'No?' The irony was heavy. 'What *would* you call it?'

Kerry lifted silk-clad shoulders, reminding herself of the game *he* had been playing his whole adult life. 'Retaliation, I suppose.'

'On someone else's behalf?'

'Why not?' she flashed. 'It was high time you had the tables turned on you!'

'Except that they weren't, were they?' he said with silky softness. 'Not for long, at any rate.'

Kerry felt the blood rush into her face. She had a struggle to come up with rightful scorn. 'As I said earlier, women arc just as vulnerable to physical desire as men—and you *are* a particularly fine specimen. Pure weakness on my part, I have to admit, but the best laid plans, and so on.'

'Whatever you like to call it, we both enjoyed it,' came the smooth return. 'Just as we'll both enjoy it again tonight.' He shook his head mockingly as she started to form a rebuttal. 'I'll carry you into the house if I have to!'

With her eyes blazing green fire, she curled a contemptuous lip. 'While the taxi driver just lets you get on with it, I suppose?'

'I doubt if it will be the first time he's witnessed marital strife.'

'We're not married.'

'He isn't to know that. Anyway, taxi drivers are very good at turning a blind eye—providing they're well rewarded.'

'It all comes down to money in the end, doesn't it?' Kerry spat back, incensed beyond measure by the cool composure. 'I'm surprised you don't offer to pay *me*!'

He gave a short laugh. 'What's your price?'

The calculated cruelty of it was like having a bucket of cold water thrown directly into her face. She turned abruptly away from him, her throat dry and aching and her chest as tight as a drum. How had she ever allowed

herself to become involved in any way with this man?
she wondered numbly. She had known what he was but
she had still stuck her head in the noose. Irrational
wasn't in it!

There were lights on at the house, although Mrs
Ralston was seeing in the New Year with friends of her
own. Kerry got out of the cab without urging, unwilling
to put the threat Lee had made to the test. Not that she
intended accepting the rest of it, she told herself fiercely
as he paid off the driver. Whatever else he might be
capable of, she doubted if rape was a possibility.

He made no attempt to touch her as they went up the
steps, opening the door and indicating that she should
precede him, his face devoid of expression.

'Do you want a drink?' he asked in the hall.

Kerry shook her head, girding herself for what would
come next.

'Well, I need one,' he said. 'You know where to go.'

He went into the drawing room, leaving her standing
there uncertainly. It took the memory of a key in the
door of the bedroom she had been allocated to jerk her
into movement. Locks could be broken, of course, but
he wouldn't go that far. Certainly not with Mrs Ralston
due home any time.

Her memory hadn't failed her. She locked the heavy
mahogany door securely and leaned against it for a moment or two to steady her nerves, feeling a sudden insane
desire to laugh. Pure hysterics, she told herself. Nothing
about this situation was in the least bit funny.

Estelle, for instance, was going to be left in the lurch
because there was no way she could continue coming
here now. What she was going to tell her, she had no
idea. Not the truth, for certain.

The agency would require explanations, too. They had
a reputation for reliability to keep up. If she couldn't
come up with a plausible reason for leaving halfway

through a job there was a very good chance that she
would be given her marching orders.

If she'd had the strength of mind to stick to her original purpose none of this would have happened, she
thought ruefully. Better still if she had steered clear of
Lee altogether. Some might say she deserved all she'd
got. They wouldn't be far wrong either.

It seemed like tempting providence to get undressed.
Sitting on the bed, she waited for the footsteps along the
landing—for the doorknob to turn. Only when half an
hour had passed with neither sign nor sound did she
finally accept that he wasn't coming. The game, so far
as he was concerned, was obviously over.

CHAPTER TEN

AWAKE at seven after a fitful sleep, Kerry was up and dressed by twenty past—hoping to leave the house before Lee surfaced. It would still leave the problem of what she was going to tell Estelle but she wouldn't be back until the following day, which gave her time to come up with something.

She was gathering her things together when the knock came on the door.

'We have to talk,' said Lee shortly. 'Better if we do it here and now.'

Kerry caught a glimpse of herself in the mirror as she straightened, aware that she looked decidedly drawn about mouth and eyes. Her hair was a mess, too—for what it mattered. Whatever attraction she had held for Lee was as dead as the year just gone. He couldn't have made that plainer.

She drew in a steadying breath before she went to open the door, trying to turn the key in the lock soundlessly. That she'd failed was apparent from the sardonicism in the grey eyes when he came into view. Fully dressed himself in close-fitting black chinos and blue cotton shirt—open at the throat on a triangle of dark hair—he looked untouched by any of last night's events.

'I decided to forgo the pleasure,' he said. 'Sorry to have disappointed you.' He gave her no time to form a come-back. 'It occurred to me that you might be considering walking out on my mother. I don't intend letting that happen.'

'I really don't see how you can stop me,' she returned tersely.

'Not forcibly, perhaps,' he agreed. 'What I *could* do is see to it that Profiles doesn't use you again.'

Kerry gazed at him in silence for a long moment, registering the implacability in the line of his mouth. This was the Lee Hartford his business rivals would know—coolly controlled, ruthless if need be. It was a wasted effort, she knew, but she made it anyway, her tone cutting.

'What makes you think you've that much power?'

The smile was derisive. 'If you doubt it there's one way of finding out.'

Kerry didn't doubt it. Not for a minute. She made a helpless little gesture. 'Surely I'm the last person you want in the house?'

'Why?' he asked. 'Because I'm likely to find it difficult to keep my hands off you?' He ran a glance over the curves revealed by the cream wool skirt and matching V-necked top, his lip curling. 'I'm not going to try making out that I wouldn't get any satisfaction from having you again, but it would be short-lived. What I will have is your word that you'll stay till the book is finished or my mother loses interest—whichever comes first.'

Kerry tilted her chin and gave him back look for look. 'How exactly would you propose explaining why we're no longer on friendly—if that's the word—terms?'

'We don't,' he said. 'We keep a civil front, and leave her to assume a simple loss of interest in any closer relationship.'

'So unusual for you, of course!'

The sarcasm drew a dangerous spark. 'Don't push it!'

'Such a fragile thing, the male ego,' she mocked, too intent on retaliation to heed the warning. 'Just can't take being used as a mere sex object yourself, can you, Lee?'

The spark flared momentarily then died, leaving an icy contempt. 'I'll phone for a taxi,' he said. 'The sooner you're out of here the better.'

Kerry turned back shakily into the room as he moved

away, aware of having come very close to breaking that
control of his—with results she didn't care to contemplate. The sooner she was out of here the better, indeed!

Carrying the overnight case, and with the dress and
coat she had worn the night before draped over her arm
in the protective cover, she went downstairs some fifteen
minutes later to find Lee waiting in the hall. There was
no sign of Mrs Ralston, thank heaven. Things were bad
enough without facing the housekeeper's curiosity.

With his face set and eyes as cold as ice, he watched
her approach.

'If you were thinking of cutting out on your own,
think again,' he said brusquely.

'I hadn't considered it,' Kerry lied.

'Just as well. The cab will be here in a few minutes.
You can phone my mother tomorrow and find out when
she wants you to come in. And don't make the mistake
of thinking I won't keep my word if you try backing
out,' he added hardily.

Kerry put everything she knew into keeping her own
tone as coldly collected. 'I'll finish the job. All I ask is
that we stay out of each other's way.'

The dark head inclined. 'Where possible. Where not,
we'll just have to handle when it happens.' He cocked
an ear. 'That sounds like the cab now. Give me your
case.'

She handed it over without protest, walking out
through the door ahead of him and down the steps to the
waiting vehicle. Lee put the suitcase in the back with
her, gave her a brief nod and turned to go back into the
house. The door closed on him as the taxi pulled away.

Hollow inside, Kerry gazed unseeingly out of the window. It was all her own fault, of course. She shouldn't
have got involved with him to start with. The only hurt
he'd suffered was to his damnable male pride, whereas
she...

She cut off that train of thought abruptly. It was over.

No point in dwelling on it. What she had to do now was pick up the pieces and get on with her life.

The flat was no more welcoming than it had been the day before. Even with the gas fire lit and a couple of lamps turned on against the winter greyness, it felt little better. Jane wouldn't be back until the following evening, which left a lot of hours to get through.

Kerry had already decided not to tell Jane about her own early return and subsequent events. It would be easier all round to have her believe that the affair had petered out quite naturally over the holiday.

Not caring to put Lee's threat to the test, she phoned Estelle on the Sunday afternoon—to find her more than ready to get back to the memoirs.

'I've been doing a lot of reminiscing over the break,' the older woman admitted. She gave a chuckle. 'I could get a whole chapter out of one period alone, but if the rather well-known party involved didn't take exception his wife probably would!' There was a pause, a change of tone. 'Tell me to mind my own business, if you like, but have you and Lee had a row?'

Thankful that they were speaking over the telephone and not face to face, Kerry tried to sound suitably surprised by the question. 'What makes you think we might have?'

'Well, I know you spent the night here New Year's Eve, but according to Mrs Ralston you left very early yesterday morning— and on your own. Lee wouldn't have let you go like that if everything was all right between you.'

She should have known the housekeeper would spill the beans, thought Kerry ruefully. 'I'm sorry,' was all she could think of to say. 'It must look very underhanded to you.'

'My dear, it's Lee's house and you're two adult people. I'd be the last one to censure you. What does concern me is what Lee could have done to make you walk out on him the way you did. Mrs Ralston said you were obviously very upset.'

'Mrs Ralston wasn't even there when I left,' Kerry returned, wondering where the woman had been skulking. 'I wasn't upset. It was a mutual decision to call it a day.'

'Then *I'm* the one who's sorry.' Estelle sounded genuinely regretful. 'I had high hopes for the two of you.' She paused again. 'How do you feel about continuing to work for me under the circumstances?'

'Fine.' Kerry could only wonder at her mastery of the easy lie. 'As you just said, we're two adult people. There's no reason why we should find things awkward.'

'Obviously not.' There was a hint of irony in her voice. 'Tomorrow, then.'

That was one hurdle over, thought Kerry dully, replacing the receiver. Maintaining the same attitude when Lee himself was present was going to be a great deal harder.

It was gone eight when Jane finally arrived.

'I'm dead!' she exclaimed, dropping her suitcase and sinking into the nearest chair. 'Didn't get to bed till five this morning, then a crowd of us went out to lunch and got thoroughly tanked up again. My head feels as if it's coming off!'

'Better take some aspirin,' Kerry advised. 'You'll need to be fit for work tomorrow.'

'Ugh, don't remind me! The very thought of getting up at the crack of dawn...' Jane left it there, glancing across at her friend with a wry grimace. 'Anyway, enough about me. How was your Christmas and New Year?'

Kerry gave a light shrug. 'Fine.'

'Just that?'

'What else? Harrogate isn't exactly a Mecca of entertainment.'

'You've got friends up there. You must have done something!'

'Nothing out of the ordinary. It's very much of a family occasion.'

'Hmm.' Jane studied her thoughtfully, obviously not wholly deceived. 'Did Lee get in touch?'

An outright denial beyond her, Kerry settled for a half-truth instead. 'He phoned to say Happy Christmas.'

'Better than nothing, I suppose. Did he give you a Christmas present before you left?'

This time it was simpler to lie outright. 'No.'

Jane pulled a face. 'Tightwad!'

'I didn't *want* anything from him,' Kerry said sharply. 'It was hardly that kind of relationship. And, before you ask, no, I shan't be seeing him again. Not privately, at any rate. There's no future in it.' She got abruptly to her feet. 'I'll make some coffee.'

Jane let her go without further comment, although her expression spoke volumes. Sympathy was the last thing Kerry wanted—from any source. She had no one to blame but herself.

Dreading the initial meeting next morning, she knew a temporary relief on arriving at the house to find that Lee had already left. He would have to be faced some time, of course, and it wasn't going to get any easier, but any reprieve was welcome.

Estelle got straight down to work with no mention of the previous day's conversation. As she had said, she had plenty to relate—and all of it highly diverting. Lee aside, the job was a gravy train, Kerry acknowledged— if only she *could* put Lee aside.

Intending to have her transcribing finished and be out of the study before he came home, she was dismayed to hear his voice in the hall before she was even halfway through. A moment later he came storming into the study in a cold fury that totally unnerved her.

'If you think *that's* going to hold any sway in the law courts you can think again!' he snapped, tossing down an opened and folded newspaper in front of her.

Kerry stared at him in bewilderment, her fingers frozen on the keyboard. 'What on earth are you talking about?'

The grey eyes were glittering slits, his jaw so tense the skin showed white about his mouth where the muscles had contracted. 'Don't try playing the wide-eyed *ingénue*!' he jerked out. 'You know damn well what I'm talking about!' He clamped a hand on the back of her neck, forcing her to look down at the newspaper in front of her. 'Read it. The item I've circled. Go on, read it!'

The ringed item was halfway down the page—just a few lines, yet heart-jerking in effect:

TYCOON TO WED SECRETARY

Company president and man-about-town, Lee Hartford, finally meets his Waterloo in the shape of redhead Kerry Pierson, straight out of the Profiles Agency drawer. The wedding will be ASAP, we're told, with just close friends and family in attendance. Congratulations to both on the happy event soon to follow. May all your troubles be little ones, Lee!

'You think *I'm* responsible for this?' Kerry got out.

'Who the devil else?' Lee removed his hand from her neck, but only to spin the chair about so that she was facing him. He leant forward with both hands planted on the arms so that she couldn't rise, his face grim and eyes no less dangerously lit. 'One thing's for certain, you're not pinning any pregnancy on *me*!'

'I'm *not* pregnant!' she flared.

'Not by me, for certain.'

'Not by anyone!' She could hardly believe what he

was intimating. 'Even if I were, I'd hardly resort to these kind of tactics!'

'So who else gave Loxley the story? Who else had anything to gain from it?' Lee wasn't giving an inch. 'What did you have in mind? An out-of-court settlement?'

The crack of her hand across his lean cheek was instinctive, anger overriding the pain in her palm. She saw his face whiten, leaving the welt standing out in bold relief for a moment before the blood rose under his skin.

She went rigid as he dragged her to her feet, her eyes widening in sudden apprehension. His hands were like steel traps on her upper arms, his mouth a thin grim line—his whole bearing indicative of controlled passion.

'I've never hit a woman in my life,' he gritted through clenched teeth, 'and I'm not about to start, whatever the temptation! What I *am* going to do is make sure you phone Loxley with a retraction right this minute!'

'I can't retract what I never said,' Kerry said fiercely. 'Why don't you ring the man yourself, and find out where he got it from?'

'Because I know where he got it from. Not that it can have been all that easy, tracking him down over the weekend.'

He let go of her abruptly and moved to the shelf where the telephone directories were stacked. He selected one and flicked through it until he found the number he was looking for, then lifted the receiver to push the appropriate keypads with force.

'It's ringing,' he said, shoving the instrument into Kerry's hand. 'If he isn't in the office tell them it's vital you reach him.'

With clenched jaw, she shook her head. 'I'm not going to take responsibility for something I didn't do!'

He hadn't closed the door when he came in. Pausing on the threshold, Estelle registered the taut atmosphere with concern.

'I heard you come in, Lee,' she said. 'What on earth happened?'

The receiver was replaced with a thud. 'This!' he said savagely, sweeping the newspaper up from the desk as his mother came forward and thrusting it at her.

Concern turned to anger as she scanned the ringed item. 'That's going too far, even by Loxley's standards!' she exploded. 'You'll sue, of course.' She looked up when her son made no answer, her expression altering again as she looked from his grim face to Kerry's rigid one. 'There's no truth in it, is there?'

'If there is *I'm* not the one involved,' said Lee emphatically. 'It's a try-on, that's all. A crude attempt at blackmail.'

'You mean Kerry...' Estelle broke off, shaking her head in disbelief as her glance went once more to the girl still standing white-faced by the desk. 'Rubbish! I'm not *that* bad a judge of character.'

'Thanks.' Kerry forced the word through stiff lips. 'Unfortunately, your son doesn't share your faith.'

Lee directed a searing glance at her. 'Is that so surprising?'

'All this because your pride got a bit dented!' she flashed back, not about to take any more from him. 'Now you know what it feels like. Sarah wasn't the only one *you* made a fool of!'

The grey eyes were like chips of ice. 'If anyone was a fool where Sarah was concerned it was me for letting it go on too long.'

'But why clear the table before you've eaten your fill?' Kerry mocked.

'Will you stop this, both of you!' Estelle was obviously at the end of her tether. 'I don't know who this Sarah is, and I don't want to know! What you should be getting to the bottom of is where Loxley got this from. And don't try telling me it's Kerry's doing again,' she added as her son started to speak, 'because I just won't believe it!'

'Then whose doing is it?' he asked flatly. 'Loxley's ethics leave a lot to be desired, but he has to have something to base his stories on. The only time he's even seen the two of us together was having lunch in Claridge's the day you sent that file along to the office. From that to this is a bit of a long shot, even for him, wouldn't you say?'

'Why don't you ask him where he got it from?' said Kerry, doing her best to regain at least some surface control of herself. 'You already dialled the number. You only have to press the redial button.'

Lee took a step towards her, pulling himself up with a visible effort. 'I'm warning you!' he said grimly. 'I'm in no mood for sarcasm!'

'I'm in no mood for *any* of this,' she returned bitterly. 'I'm not responsible for that item.' She made a shaky movement, surprised to find her legs would support her at all. 'You can do what you like about it. I'm going home.'

'You're not going anywhere,' he stated, blocking her way. 'Not until you stop lying.'

To her dismay, Kerry felt hot moisture prickling at the backs of her eyes. Tears now would rob her of what little dignity she had left. She blinked hard and fast, but to no avail. Lee curled a lip as a bead stole down her cheek.

'No waterworks, please!'

'What would you expect?' asked his mother caustically. 'You're enough to make anyone weep! Just like your father. He only ever saw things one way, too! Why don't you try considering who else might have given Loxley a call?'

'Who else would be likely to?' he responded without change of tone.

'You might try Renata, for one,' said Kerry thickly.

'She didn't like it when you walked out on her New Year's Eve.'

Just for a moment the grey eyes showed doubt, then they hardened again. 'That's ridiculous!'

'Is it?' Estelle sounded meditative. 'I'm not so sure. She only married Philip because she couldn't have you. Seeing you with Kerry would be enough to bring out the green-eye full force. You know how vindictive she can be.'

Lee looked unconvinced. 'Not enough to do something like this.'

'Don't waste your time, Estelle,' Kerry advised wearily. 'He isn't going to believe it.'

'We'll give him a few minutes on his own to think about it while you and I go and have a calming drink,' returned the older woman. 'We'll be in the drawing room when you come to your senses,' she added to her son.

Kerry allowed herself to be steered from the room by the firm hand at her back. Only when they reached the hall did she make any attempt to contest her employer's decisiveness.

'I really do appreciate your support,' she said gratefully, 'but I think it would be better all round if I left.'

'I don't want you to leave,' came the firm reply. 'Neither will Lee once he gets his mind straight. I'm not sure just what happened between you two to make him feel so vicious towards you but, whatever it was, it can surely be sorted out.' She paused, her eyes reflecting a certain doubt as they rested on the youthfully lovely face before her. 'Unless I've totally mistaken the way you feel about my son?'

The doubt disappeared at Kerry's involuntary change of expression. 'I thought not. Not that he deserves to have you feel anything good about him at all after the way he just treated you.'

'He thinks I was playing him along,' Kerry said tone-lessly.

'And were you?'

'A little, to start with. At least, that was the idea.'

'On behalf of this Sarah?'

'Yes.' Kerry gave a wan little smile. 'A ridiculous idea, I know.'

'Only worth entertaining where there was no chance at all of becoming involved yourself,' Estelle agreed. 'I felt the vibes between the two of you that very first day. You must have been aware of them, too.' She shook her head as Kerry made to speak again. 'Come and have that drink.'

Short of flatly refusing, which she didn't feel up to doing, Kerry had little choice but to accompany her employer through to the drawing room. Estelle didn't bother asking her what she wanted, just went and poured two stiff gin and tonics.

'A bit early in the day, perhaps, but I doubt if tea would be sufficiently bracing,' she said, bringing the glasses across to where Kerry had sunk reluctantly to a seat. 'Whatever Lee believes, he has no right to put you through this kind of catechism!'

Kerry made no reply. Both her head and throat ached with tension. As Lee had said, someone had to have given Kenneth Loxley the supposed information and Renata was the only candidate with a likely motive.

According to what Estelle had suggested, she had married Philip on the rebound after Lee had turned her down. Having him do it again on New Year's Eve, if only in her own covetous mind, must have made her yearn to pay out not just Lee but the woman she blamed for his defection.

It *had* to be Renata.

The gin and tonic did absolutely nothing to calm her frayed nerves, although she sipped at it dutifully under Estelle's watchful gaze. It had been more than fifteen

minutes since they had left Lee in the study. If he had
done as she said, and contacted Kenneth Loxley himself,
he should surely know by now that she wasn't the culprit.

As if in answer to her thoughts, the door opened to
admit the subject of them. Meeting the still-flinty grey
eyes, Kerry felt her heart plummet.

'He's out of town for a few days,' he said without
preamble. 'Not that I expect him to divulge his source
without encouragement, anyway.'

'You mean pay him?' Kerry asked hesitantly.

'I mean whatever's necessary to make him come
across. One way or another, I'm going to get to the bottom of it,' Lee added with hard assertion. 'And whoever
is responsible...' He left it there, the tone of his voice
alone enough to finish the sentence for him.

Kerry had had enough of the whole business. All she
wanted at that moment was to get away from the man
she had thought she loved—fool that she was! She put
down the glass and got abruptly to her feet, felt her head
suddenly spin and then everything faded.

She was lying on the sofa when she came round,
Estelle hovering anxiously over her. 'What happened?'
she asked dazedly.

'You passed out,' said the older woman. 'You only
just missed hitting your head on the coffee-table.' She
hesitated, an odd expression in her eyes. 'Are you prone
to fainting?'

Kerry shook her head, increasing the ache already
there. 'I don't remember ever doing it before in my life.'

Estelle hesitated again, obviously reluctant to say
whatever it was she was about to say. When she did
speak it was diffidently.

'Kerry, is there any chance at all that you *could* be
pregnant?'

CHAPTER ELEVEN

KERRY felt the bottom suddenly drop out of her stomach. Rejection was swift and fierce. 'No, there isn't!'

'Just a thought,' came the soothing rejoinder. 'Hormone changes can sometimes cause fainting spells, that's all.'

'Not in this instance.' Kerry pushed herself upright, shutting out the small voice trying to make itself heard. 'No chance!'

'You quite sure about that?' asked Lee from somewhere beyond the periphery of her vision, and she turned her head to see him standing at the end of the sofa in narrowed contemplation.

'Of course I'm sure!' she flung at him. 'You're conscientious enough *that* way, at least!'

The dark head inclined in sardonic acknowledgement. 'I do my best. How about you?'

Kerry bit her lip. She had had no cause to take precautions since Ray had gone out of her life, and if she'd thought about it at all that night with Lee she had been reassured by his own prudence. Considering which, there was surely no way she could be pregnant—was there?

'I gather the answer's no,' said Lee when she failed to reply.

Her chin lifted. 'What difference would it make?'

'There's such a thing as double insurance. Nothing is a hundred per cent foolproof.'

Especially when it came to a fool like her, she thought hollowly, unable to sustain anger in the face of a doubt she could no longer fully suppress. 'I'm going home,' she said in subdued tones. 'I'm sorry, Estelle, but you'll

171

have to find someone else. I can't continue coming here after this. You can do what you think fit about that, too,' she added to Lee. 'I really don't care any more.'

There was something unfathomable in his grey eyes. When he spoke again it was dispassionately. 'I'll take you.'

Already on her feet, Kerry gave him a disbelieving glance. 'Do you think I'd let you? I'll take the tube, thanks!'

His expression unyielding, he said, 'We need to talk.'

'What's left to say? You made your feelings plain enough.' Her limbs were trembling so much she could scarcely stand, the tight knot of pain inside her beginning to unwind into every part of her body. 'I don't want *anything* from you, Lee. I never did!'

'Well, you're getting a lift home, like it or not.' He shook his head as his mother made to intervene. 'This is between the two of us.'

Looking at him, Kerry knew herself beaten. He was stronger than she was all the way down the line. Whatever he had to say, it could hardly be worse than what he'd already said.

Recognising the futility, Estelle made no further protest, although she looked thoroughly upset. Sorry as she was to abandon her barely halfway through the book, Kerry consoled herself with the thought that Profiles would soon come up with a suitable replacement. Where her own employment with the agency was concerned remained to be seen. Right now she had more to worry about.

Lee didn't touch her on the way out to the car. He obviously hadn't lingered to put on an overcoat, before leaving the office—despite the bitterly cold day—and didn't bother with one now. Warm at least on the outside in her own camel coat, Kerry braced herself as he slid behind the wheel to start the engine with a flick of a lean brown wrist and pull out from the kerb.

His face in profile looked austere—so different from when he had driven her back from Harrogate three days ago. She had been in love with him then—or had imagined herself to be—which meant she had probably been viewing him through rose-coloured spectacles to start with. They were well and truly smashed now.

There was no conversation on the way. Not that Kerry felt like talking. If she had entertained any hope at all of his dumping her at the flat and driving away again it was dashed when he got out with her and locked the car.

It was still only a little after four, she saw, glancing surreptitiously at her watch as they went indoors. Jane wouldn't be home for a couple of hours at least, even more if she decided to go out straight from work.

The flat had never looked more unwelcoming. Kerry went to turn on the gas fire, nerving herself to straighten and face the tall, uncompromising figure standing waiting for her.

'So, get it off your chest,' she invited with what control she could muster.

With a penetrating gaze, he said curtly, 'When are you due?'

The bald question brought sudden flags of colour to her face—along with a repeat of the sinking sensation deep down inside. She fought to repress the feeling, refusing to let herself fully believe even for a minute that it might be true.

'I've no intention of answering that,' she said between tight lips.

'Because you're overdue?' Lee was giving no quarter. 'You must know.'

Kerry did know. She had had too much else on her mind until now to think about it, but there was no getting away from the fact that she was already several days late.

'So?' Lee obviously had no intention of letting her off the hook. 'When?'

'None of your business,' she retorted, and saw the lean features tauten still further.

'I'm making it my business!'

Her eyes jade-dark and face pale within the frame of chestnut hair, but for the spots of colour still burning high on her cheek-bones, Kerry gave him back look for look. 'According to what you said earlier, there's no way *you* could be responsible for whatever condition I might find myself in so why don't you just get out of here and leave me *alone*!'

Her voice broke on the last word. Afraid of giving way completely, she turned abruptly to make for the safety and solitude of her bedroom, tripped and almost fell as her toe caught the edge of the hearthrug. She didn't hear Lee move, but he was there before she recovered her balance, his hand snaking under her arm to pull her upright.

'You'd better sit down,' he said. 'We don't want you passing out again.'

There was every chance that he thought the last time had been put on for show, but Kerry was too distressed to care. She allowed him to put her into a seat on the nearby sofa, aware of the uncontrollable tremors running through her and knowing he must feel them, too. She couldn't bring herself to look up at him as he towered over her, instead gazing blindly at the hands tightly clasped in her lap.

'Now tell me the truth,' he demanded. '*Are* you pregnant?'

'I'm not sure.' Her voice was low, all the stuffing knocked out of her. 'I'm late, but that doesn't necessarily—'

'You mean you're often late?'

She sighed, knowing it was no use. 'No.'

'Then I'd say it's pretty likely.' Lee drew in a long slow breath, letting it out again with controlled force. 'Do you always rely on the other party for protection?'

That did bring her head up, a new spark to her eyes. 'I've told you before, I *don't* sleep around! I didn't plan on spending the night with you, believe me!'

'You didn't exactly slam the door in my face,' came the pointed rejoinder, bringing a fresh wave of heat to her cheeks.

'And I suppose if I had you'd have accepted it like the gentleman you are, of course!'

'I wouldn't have broken it down, if that's what you're implying.' He made an impatient gesture. 'This is getting us nowhere. You need to see a doctor.'

'A doctor probably couldn't verify it one way or the other at this stage,' Kerry returned unsteadily.

'I'm sure there are tests that can be done, however early.'

She eyed him in silence for a moment, wishing he would at least sit down so that she didn't feel quite so disadvantaged. 'Why should it concern you, anyway, if you're convinced that you're not responsible?'

'I'm in the picture, whether I like it or not,' came the harsh return. 'Loxley's little piece made sure of that.'

'And you still think I gave it to him, of course.'

A muscle jerked suddenly in the firm jawline as he regarded the striking, wide-browed face upturned to his. 'I just find it difficult to believe that anyone else would have done it.'

'Renata being above such tactics, I suppose.' Kerry kept her voice as level as she could. 'If what your mother said was true she'd already suffered rejection once at your hands. Having you turn her down again New Year's Eve could have been the last straw. What better way to pay you out than to give someone like Kenneth Loxley that story?'

Lee considered her narrowly with his hands thrust into his trouser pockets, obviously weighing the points she had made. When he spoke it was with somewhat less brusqueness.

'What exactly do you reckon I turned down New Year's Eve?'

'What she was so openly offering. I wasn't the only one who noticed. Philip knew it, too. He also knows she was in love with you when she married him.'

Lee gave a short hard laugh. 'What Renata knows about love wouldn't fill a pinhead! Phil unfortunately let his hormones rule his head, but there'll come a time when he's had enough of her, too.'

The sentiments were too candidly expressed to be anything but genuine. In spite of everything, Kerry took some comfort from the knowledge that the other woman was so contemptuously regarded.

'I didn't contact Kenneth Loxley,' she said softly. 'It wouldn't have occurred to me, even if I'd known...'

Her voice trailed away as the possibility—no, probability—came back to haunt her. She wouldn't be the first to finish up that way, by any means, but it didn't help to know it. She daren't contemplate her father's reactions.

'It's my problem, anyway,' she got out. 'There's no need for you to bother about it.'

'If you're having my child there's every need for me to bother about it!' returned Lee abrasively. 'First, we're going to get you to a gynaecologist and make sure. Second—' He cut off there with a brief shake of his head. 'We'll cover that later. It's too late to start ringing for appointments now but I'll sort something out first thing in the morning.'

Kerry forced herself to look him straight in the eye, steeling her heart against the pain. 'Does that mean you accept my word that you're the only possible...candidate?'

'It means,' he said, 'that I'm not prepared to turn my back on the possibility.'

'Lee.' There was a hard obstruction in her throat, making speech difficult. 'I might have started the whole thing on Sarah's behalf but it wasn't her I was thinking of that night.'

'I can believe it,' came the unmoved reply. 'By then you'd realised there were benefits to be exploited on your own behalf.'

'If that was true why would you have to talk me into continuing the affair?'

He gave a dry laugh. 'I'd already told you how I reacted to a challenge. You judged the performance just about right all the way down the line. Where you went wrong was in letting Renata's antics get to you. If you'd kept your cool New Year's Eve who knows where we might have finished up?'

'The same place we *have* finished up,' Kerry said flatly, abandoning any hope of getting through to him. 'If I'm pregnant now I was pregnant then so losing my cool, as you put it, made little difference in the end.'

Lee made an abrupt movement, his face closed again. 'I don't see any point in going over the same ground. I'll phone you in the morning.'

Sitting where he had left her as the door closed quietly behind him, Kerry fought the depression that threatened to overcome her. It wasn't totally certain yet that she was pregnant at all

Whether she was or not she had lost any chance there might ever have been of having Lee come to feel something real and lasting for her. He would take financial care of things if it turned out to be necessary because he had no way of proving beyond a shadow of a doubt that he wasn't answerable, but all she would be to him was a liability.

Jane got home at six-thirty, in too much of a rush to change and get out again to notice anything amiss. Kerry spent the evening watching television—or with the set turned on at least—and went to bed at ten, reluctant to face her flatmate again. She would have to put her in the picture to a certain extent, if only to explain why she

was no longer working for Estelle, but she wasn't ready
to do it tonight.

Emotionally exhausted, she slept through till eight,
emerging from her room to find Jane on the verge of
leaving for work.

'Some people live a cushy life!' remarked the other
girl in mock envy. 'If you've nothing on tonight how
about making up a foursome with a friend of Drew's?'
she added, biting into a piece of toast while struggling
into her coat. 'Name's Steve. Twenty-six, and a real live-
wire, according to Drew. Could be fun.'

Kerry shook her head, trying to sound casual about it.
'Not tonight, thanks. I'm washing my hair.'

'No point moping around after lover-boy,' came the
candid response. 'You need to get out and forget him.
Think about it, anyway. If not tonight then tomorrow.'

She had a whole lot more to think about than going
on some blind date, Kerry reflected as her friend rushed
out the door with the half-eaten piece of toast in her
hand. She only hoped she wasn't going to have too much
time to do it in.

The promised phone call came shortly after nine
o'clock. Lee sounded brisk and businesslike.

'You're seeing the man at eleven. I'll be over to pick
you up at ten-thirty.'

'Just tell me where to go,' Kerry requested. 'I can
make my own way there.'

'I said I'd pick you up.' The tone was unequivocal.
'Have you had breakfast yet?'

The question took her by surprise. 'I haven't got round
to having anything yet,' she said blankly.

'Good. It's apparently best if you take a sample before
you have a drink.'

It was on the tip of her tongue to ask what sample,
but she bit it back. There was a time and place for flip-
pancy and this was neither.

She replaced the receiver before he could cut her off,

standing there for a moment calming herself down. There was absolutely no reason for Lee to accompany her—she would be only too delighted to tell him it was a false alarm. Not that she had any choice in the matter, it appeared.

Still tired, she had to force herself to get ready for the coming ordeal and opted for a suit in tan wool, with a long-line jacket and a short skirt that made her legs look even longer. Her hair she clipped back into her nape with a tortoiseshell slide, bringing her cheek-bones into sharp relief. Even with make-up on, she still looked drained, she thought listlessly, viewing herself in the mirror. She applied a little more blusher but that didn't seem to help much either.

It still needed five minutes to the half-hour when the bell rang. Dressed for work in a dark grey pinstripe, Lee looked her over with a jaundiced eye.

'Ready?' was all he said.

Turning to get her handbag from the nearby chair, Kerry felt a sudden wave of nausea. She fought it down grimly, trying to tell herself it was just nerves—knowing full well that it wasn't. The test was just a formality. She was pregnant all right. The sooner she faced up to it the better.

They were in the car before she allowed herself to think beyond the word itself to what was actually growing inside her—scarcely more than a dot as yet, but scheduled to become a complete little person. She felt the first stirrings of mother love. If she couldn't have Lee then at least she would have his child.

The appointment was in Harley Street—naturally. Lee parked the car and accompanied her up to the first-floor reception, taking a seat while she went through to see the consultant.

He put no immediate question when she came out again some twenty minutes later, just led the way downstairs again. Only when they were back in the car did he show any sign of impatience.

'Don't keep me in suspense,' he jerked out. 'What's the verdict?'

'The test was positive,' Kerry said levelly. 'The way they work it out I'm almost five weeks gone, although it's really only just over two. Simple at this stage, anyway, apparently.'

Lee gave her a long, hard look. 'What is?'

'Abortion.'

His teeth snapped together, his whole face registering fierce repudiation. 'You'll abort no child of mine!' he said forcefully. 'I'll lock you up for the duration if I have to!'

'I wouldn't contemplate it,' Kerry assured him. 'I want this baby.'

His fierceness gave way to something far less easily defined. For a long, pulse-racing moment he studied her face. When he spoke it was on an uncharacteristically tentative note. 'You're sure about that?'

'Yes.' She could say it with certainty. 'It might not be the ideal situation but, providing you're prepared to contribute to his or her welfare, I'm sure we'll manage fine. Others bring up a child single-handed so why shouldn't—?'

'If you think I'm going to step aside and let you do that you can damn well think again!' Lee jerked through freshly tautened lips. 'I'm having *my* name on that birth certificate!'

Kerry could feel her heart pounding against her ribcage. Her stomach muscles were so tense they hurt. She said thickly, 'Last night you weren't even all that convinced that you're the father.'

'That was last night—this is now. I accept responsibility all the way. The first thing we're going to do is get a licence.' The words were clipped, decisive. 'We're going to bring up *this* child in a proper environment!'

Faced with this wholly unanticipated development, Kerry gazed at him in confusion. He was talking about marriage—and not in any temporary sense either. '*We're* going to bring up this child,' he'd said. That meant years, not weeks or months.

Years of marriage to a man who didn't love her, came the sobering thought. Could she stand that, even for the child's sake? No matter how resolved he was to take control of the situation he couldn't force her into doing anything she didn't want to do. She had a life of her own, a will of her own.

'I'm not going to marry you, Lee,' she said with surprising steadiness. 'If I ever marry at all it will be for love, not expedience.'

'Then you'd better start learning,' he returned grimly.

Kerry held her tongue as he started the car and slammed it into gear, recognising the futility of any further verbal dissent. She wasn't the one who needed to learn how to love, she thought wryly; she had been there almost from the beginning. What she couldn't take was his lack of it.

He drove her straight back to the flat, his face set in lines that brooked no contention as he took her by the arm to lead her indoors. Only when they were safely inside, with the door closed, did he let go of her, his eyes challenging her to try getting past him.

'You're going to marry me, Kerry,' he stated roughly. 'If I can't persuade you one way then we'll try another.'

She backed off as he moved purposefully towards her but she didn't get far. He hauled her to him, his mouth a bruising force she couldn't escape. After the first rigid second or two she no longer wanted to escape. What she wanted was what he was giving her—no choice.

Still kissing her, he slid an arm under her knees, lifted her up and carried her through to her room to lay her on the bed. Kerry slid her arms over the broad shoulders as

he came down on her, feeling the leashed power in
him—the potent weight of his arousal.

The blood was drumming in her ears, her whole body
fired by the need to be closer still, to be part of him
again—a rush of emotion so intense she could scarcely
contain it.

He undressed her swiftly, surely, pausing to run his
lips over her quivering abdomen before straightening to
strip off his own clothing. His eyes were glowing with
an inner fire when he lowered himself to her again, his
hands possessive.

Kerry buried her face in his broad chest, running the
tip of her tongue through the wiry tangle of dark hair to
taste the salt on his skin. Her thighs parted to take him,
her long legs wrapping about him as he penetrated the
molten centre of her body and filled the void he had left
in her life these past weeks.

'You're going to marry me,' Lee repeated softly some
incalculable time later when the world had steadied
again. 'We're going to be a family, Kerry. A complete
family. The kind I never really knew.'

'Can it work,' she asked huskily, 'without love to hold
it together?'

He looked down at her—at the spread of chestnut hair
across the pillow, the pure lines of her face and vulnerable mouth—and his jaw contracted. 'We'll make it
work! I've waited too long for someone I could feel this
way about to give up now.'

'Exactly how *do* you feel?' Kerry whispered, hardly
able to believe that he meant what he appeared to be
saying.

The strong mouth slanted wryly. 'You really want my
head on a platter, don't you?'

Green eyes took on new depths as they looked long
and hard into grey, uncertainty giving way to flooding
relief. 'No,' she said. 'I want you just the way you are.'
Her voice had a tremor in it. 'If you only knew how

wretched I've been this last couple of days. I'd have given anything to cancel what I tried making out New Year's Eve. I was using Sarah as an excuse all along. I wanted you from the very first minute I set eyes on you.'

A spark of humour lit the grey gaze. 'You certainly went all out not to show it!'

'For what good it did me. You knew what I was feeling.'

'I knew we were both of us of the same mind with regard to the sexual side,' Lee agreed. 'What I wasn't prepared for was what you made me feel besides that.' He bent his head to put his lips to her temple where the hair clung damply, the gentle caress more meaningful at that moment than any more passionate gesture.

'I'd never fallen all the way before. I could hardly believe it could happen so fast. When we spent the night together I thought you were beginning to feel the same way. Waking up to what I did was a real kick in the gut.'

'*I* thought that was all you were interested in,' Kerry admitted. 'I was trying to make out that it didn't mean any more to me than it did to you.' She brought both hands up to cup the lean face, loving the texture of his skin, the warmth and weight of his body over her— feeling the stirring between her thighs as he came to life again. 'You're sure, aren't you?'

He gave a low laugh, moving slowly and subtly against her. 'Does *this* leave you in any doubt?'

'I'm talking about love, not lust,' she retorted thickly. 'Do you really know the difference?'

'No doubt at all.' He dropped his head to find her mouth, cherishing it with a tenderness that moved her immeasurably. 'I love you, I want you and I need you,' he murmured against her lips. 'More than I ever needed anyone or anything in my life before. Kerry...'

He got no further as she closed off his mouth with hers. Passion flared swiftly between them, too overwhelming to be denied a second longer. Made for each other, was Kerry's last sentient thought as he filled her once more with his vibrant masculinity.

It was gone two when they finally emerged from the bedroom. Dressed again and outwardly in command of herself, Kerry made coffee for them both and brought the tray over to the sofa where Lee had seated himself at her instigation.

'I could rustle up some lunch,' she offered, handing him a cup. 'Nothing fancy, but there's plenty of eggs, mushrooms, and so on.'

He shook his head. 'I'm not hungry. Not for food, at any rate,' he added with a glint that brought an answering smile to her lips.

'I think we've fed the inner man enough for one day.'

The glint became a gleam. 'You're not thinking of imposing restrictions, I hope.'

'As if,' she returned, 'you'd let me if I tried!'

'As if you'd want me to.' He viewed her flushed face and sparkling eyes with satisfaction. 'You're as gluttonous as I am, thank heaven!'

'There's more to marriage than sex,' Kerry pointed out, her laughter dimming a little as uncertainty raised its head once more. 'I'm going to be fat and ugly in a few months. How will you feel then?'

'You couldn't be ugly under any circumstances.' Both voice and expression had softened. 'Especially not when you're carrying my child. I love you, Kerry. Don't ever doubt that.'

She searched the hard-boned features, looking for and finding some reassurance in the steady grey regard—but still not wholly convinced. 'But would you be contemplating marriage if it weren't for the baby?'

'I was contemplating marriage when I came to fetch you back from Harrogate,' he said. 'I planned on making New Year's Eve the time and place, but you know what they say about the best-laid plans.' He made a wry ges-

ture. 'When you made out you'd just been leading me
on in retaliation for what you thought I'd done to Sarah
I wanted to hurt you. Luckily for both of us, I came to
my senses in time.'

'Sarah told me you'd led her to believe you were going to be married.' Kerry kept her tone carefully neutral.

'Not true.' There was no undue emphasis in the statement, which somehow served to make it even more be-
lievable. 'You either take my word for it or hers.'

When it came down to it, there was no contest. 'I take
yours, of course,' she said. 'Just as I hope you'll take
mine when I tell you you need never have any doubts
as to whose child it is.'

'I don't.' Lee was smiling again. 'We'll need to tell
your parents first but there's no reason why we shouldn't
be married right away. After all, we've already had the
press announcement.'

Kerry looked at him questioningly. 'You're going to
let that piece stand?'

'I can hardly sue for libel under the circumstances.'

'But you still don't think I...?'

He put a finger to her lips, cutting off the words with
a rueful expression. 'If I'd been thinking straight yesterday, I'd have realised right away who the culprit was.
Just Renata's style—*and* she knows Kenneth Loxley
personally.' Humour reasserted itself. 'She'll have the
shock of her life when she realises she was telling the
truth for once.'

'But people are still going to see it as a needs-must
wedding,' Kerry said wryly.

'So what if they do? We'll know they're wrong, and
that's all that matters. We're going to be together a long
time,' Lee added firmly, seeing the doubt still lingering
in her eyes. 'How we started isn't important—it's how
we carry on. One thing we're going to be doing is finding a place out of town with a proper garden and space

for kids to play. Other people commute—there's no reason why I shouldn't join them.'

Kerry was all for the plural. Both she and Lee lacked siblings. This child of theirs wasn't going to be so deprived. She liked the idea of a house in the country, too, but there were other factors to consider.

'If you sell the house here what about your mother?' she asked diffidently.

'Mother,' he said with purpose, 'will be living her own life back in the world she knows best. All she needs is a little more persuasion from all sides. You and Gregory can help supply it.'

'You think persuasion is going to work?'

'If it doesn't I'll try eviction.'

'A real hard man!' Kerry teased.

He quirked an eyebrow. 'Would you have me any other way?'

She pulled a face at him, feeling the desire building inside her again as she viewed the firm, masculine features—remembering the pleasure that mouth of his could afford. She saw his expression slowly change, his eyes acquire that pulse-racing spark.

'A woman after my own heart,' he said softly, drawing her to him.

Always, she thought as his lips claimed hers once more.

Take 2 bestselling love stories FREE

Plus get a FREE surprise gift!

Special Limited-Time Offer

Mail to Harlequin Reader Service®

3010 Walden Avenue
P.O. Box 1867
Buffalo, N.Y. 14240-1867

YES! Please send me 2 free Harlequin Presents® novels and my free surprise gift. Then send me 6 brand-new novels every month, which I will receive months before they appear in bookstores. Bill me at the low price of $3.12 each plus 25¢ delivery and applicable sales tax, if any*. That's the complete price, and a saving of over 10% off the cover prices—quite a bargain! I understand that accepting the books and gift places me under no obligation ever to buy any books. I can always return a shipment and cancel at any time. Even if I never buy another book from Harlequin, the 2 free books and the surprise gift are mine to keep forever.

106 HEN CH69

Name	(PLEASE PRINT)	
Address	Apt. No.	
City	State	Zip

This offer is limited to one order per household and not valid to present Harlequin Presents® subscribers. *Terms and prices are subject to change without notice. Sales tax applicable in N.Y.

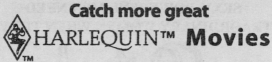